The Kin of Ata Are Waiting for You

Formerly published as *The Comforter*

Dorothy Bryant

Moon Books / Random House

Co-published by: Random House, Inc.
                     201 East 50th Street
                     New York, N.Y. 10022

     and:

                     Moon Books
                     Post Office Box 9223
                     Berkeley, California 94709

Moon Books is an independent women's publishing company operating out of San Francisco, California, with distribution through Random House, Inc., in New York. We are committed to making a wide variety of feminist material available in the general market.

Illustrations by Edidt Geever

Library of Congress Cataloging-in-Publication Data

Bryant, Dorothy, 1930–
    The Kin of Ata are Waiting for You.

First published in 1971 under title: The Comforter.
    I. Title.
PZ4.B91477Ki3 (PS3552.R878) 813'.5'4 76-8195
ISBN 0-394-40729-6
ISBN 0-679-77843-8

Random House website address: http://www.randomhouse.com/

Printed in the United States of America on acid-free paper
98765

". . . and the Comforter . . .
shall teach you all things
and bring all things
to your remembrance."

One

"Bastard! You son of a bitch! Bastard!"

I was almost bored. She stood in front of me like a woman out of one of my books. I had a sudden thought that I might have invented her: long legs, small waist, full breasts half covered by tossed blonde hair. I must have smiled because she swung at me again. I caught her wrist, and she made a stifled sound of anger, almost a growl.

"Put your clothes on and get out," I told her.

She went on screaming at me. I sat on the edge of the bed and watched her. Her breasts were full, but they hung loose, like bags over a torso on which I could count every rib. The pubic hair told the true color of her bleached head: mousy brown. Her skin, breaking through her smeared make-up, was blotchy.

"I exist!" she was screaming. "I'm a person!"

I yawned and looked at the clock. Four a.m. "No," I told her. "I invented you, or you tried to invent yourself, right out of my latest book. But some of the details got . . ."

She lunged at me. She took me by surprise, and I fell

back on the bed with her on top of me. She gave a little jump onto her knees and started digging her fingernails into my face. She almost straddled me, but one knee pressed down on my chest. Her hair and her breasts dangled over my eyes, merging like the slack dugs of some obscene animal. Her breath smelled sour, wine and pot mingling in a sickly smell that turned my stomach.

I tried to grab her wrists, but they were slick with sweat and kept slipping away from me. She was stonger than I expected, and she was hurting me, taking long slashes at my face, aiming at my eyes.

Finally I grabbed her by the shoulders and stretched her away from me at arms length. Her fingernails clawed the air an inch from my nose. I pushed, and she landed against the wall behind the bed, making a couple of thick slapping noises as she hit the wall, then bouncing back at me, her eyes and mouth wide, her claws flailing. As she fell toward me, I stretched out my arm and caught her by the throat.

It wouldn't have happened if we hadn't been stoned. And if it hadn't been four o'clock in the morning. And if it hadn't been for the nightmare. But the nightmare had been especially bad that week, and I'd had hardly any sleep, trying to keep it from me.

It didn't feel like murder. It was all unreal, like a scene from one of my books. Or she was like a phantom from my nightmare, the phantom I held off with my eyes closed, afraid to look. I wasn't real either. Nothing could be real at four o'clock in the morning. I might wake up anytime, sweating and shaking, and take another pill to push me to a level beyond or below nightmare.

It had been quiet for a long time when I gradually came

to myself. The first thing I realized was that I was cold. Then I felt the ache in my outstretched arm. I looked down my arm to where my hand gripped her throat, pressing her against the wall. My arm ached because she was heavy, hanging in my grip like a wet doll. Her eyes and mouth were still wide, but her face was dark, and she was quiet. I let go and she slid down the wall, crouched as if she would sit resting against it, then toppled over to one side. I could tell by the way she lay there that she was dead. There was something inhuman, deadlike, in the way her body crumpled.

I looked at the clock: 4:15. Was that all? I thought a lifetime must have passed. It had, of course. In those few minutes, my lifetime, all that my life was, had passed away, had died with . . . it took me a few minutes to remember her name . . . with Connie.

But I wasn't thinking of my life, past or future. If I was thinking at all, it was of escape, of running away. And that wasn't really thinking. It was instinct. Pure panic vibrated through my knees, widening the huge, windy void at the center of my body.

I put my clothes on. I ran out to the garage, got into my car, and drove off.

I didn't know where I was going. I had some idea of getting far away before the sun came up, before the light shone through the glass doors at the end of my bedroom, and lit up the brittle blonde hair falling over the bloated face that leaned against the baseboard.

That part of me saw the body. That part of me drove.

Another part of me stood off watching, and after a while that second part of me started to talk. You fool. You did it now. You had everything. You had everything you always wanted. You were at the top. There was nothing left that you could want. And you threw it away.

I shook my head and turned onto the freeway. Going south. That was all right. Going somewhere. Anywhere. Going away.

Don't run away, the other part of me said. Go back. Take the body and dump it somewhere.

You read too many of your own books. (Was it another part of me, arguing? How many ways was I split?) You've been seen with her. People know. You don't go anywhere without being recognized. They'd connect it with you.

All right, that's why you pay a lawyer. Call Spanger. He's gotten you out of messes before. Temporary insanity. Get your psychiatrist in on it. He can tell about the nightmares. You're a sick man.

A killer or sick. All the same. It's over. You had it all and threw it away. Now they won't read your books anymore, they'll read you, in the morning paper, every stupid voyeur who ever masturbated to your books will take you with his morning coffee and lick his lips.

Where are you going to go?

Did you bring any money?

How far can you get without more gas?

The nagging voices buzzed like flies around my body. My silent body answered nothing, thought nothing. It heard without listening and kept driving.

I don't remember turning off the freeway. I don't remember the road I took to the mountain. I don't remember the ascent. There was nothing but the whining voices inside me and the still, stolid body driving.

I don't remember the curve.

It was only when the car began to roll over, when my

body driving it no longer drove it, that I realized I'd turned too sharply, skidded, and gone off the edge of the road.

It all happened with incredible slowness. The car shuddered on the edge, then rolled over. I gripped the wheel as my foot lost the pedal and my head bounced against the roof. For one eternal second the car floated through the air. Then it hit, bouncing on its side, shattering the windows, rattling like tin cans on gravel. Then it rolled, and rolled, grating and scraping, rolling, as within the car I spun and crashed like cargo broken loose, until I saw the broken door fly off and felt myself bounced through the opening into space.

I remember that moment when the car spewed me out, that moment of floating in space. It was in that instant that I first realized I might die, in that instant that my whole being unified into the realization of my own death, not as a theoretical possibility or a far distant probability, not as a word unimagined or repressed, but as a palpable thing, a permanent state. My death. I knew, not with the blind panic of my flight from Connie's death, but with a clear and rational fear that burst on me like the bright sunlight dawning on that mountainside. I knew that my death would be a permanent plunge into the nightmare. I heard myself scream, not in fear of what might happen, but in the sure horror of knowing.

I had never screamed before. It was not a scream, but more like a great howl into which my falling body melted. And then the nightmare swallowed me.

My eyes are shut. I am surrounded by shadowy shapes. They close in. I must fight them off. But I must not look at them. How can I fight if I can't see them? I must run, but they are all around me. I might run into the grasp of one. Don't look at them. They are closer. I feel their breath on me. I throw out my arms to hold them off. But they will swallow my hands. I spin around with my arms outstretched, clearing a safe circle around me. I turn and turn, I spin so the shadows cannot come closer, faster, so they cannot catch my hands. I make a great wind circling round me. I spin, faster and faster until I am dizzy. I am dizzy. I am falling. I fall. I fall, and they are on me. They have me.

My eyes opened. I was not dead. It was all just another nightmare. The murder, the drive, the accident, all a refinement on the old nightmare. For a while I lay still, breathing deeply, gratefully. I did not want to move. In a moment, I would roll over, look at the clock and take another pill. But not yet. I wanted to lie still and safe, in my own bed, in my house. In a moment I would sit up and laugh and write down my dream for the psychiatrist. It was a good one. He would dig into it like a kid making mud pies.

I started to roll over, but the shock of pain made me gasp, feeling as if knives had dug deep into every part of my body involved in the move. I lay still again. It had not been a dream. I was hurt, very badly hurt. I made tentative moves, first in my fingers, then my hands. By the time I tried my arms, I again felt the stabs of pain telegraphed throughout my body. I knew there was some very good reason not to move my right leg. A mere twitch of a toe warned me that something was very wrong there. I raised my hand to my face. It felt wet, and it stung when I touched it. My hand was stiff, my fingers raw.

Now even without movement I felt the pain of the scrapes and bruises covering my body. My leg must be broken, I thought. And with every breath, I knew that I must have cracked most of the ribs on my right side. My slight movements had activated a smashing pain in my skull. I felt almost as if even blinking my eyes would crack my head wide open. I groaned, and I heard a soft rustling sound near me. Then it stopped. Someone had been there and was gone. Where? Who? Where was I? I could see nothing. Everything was absolute blackness and stillness. Brain damage, I thought; blind and deaf. Perhaps I was mute as well. I should try to speak. I hesitated for a minute, stupidly wondering what to say, as if it mattered. Finally I said, "Hello." It came out in a sharp whisper through my dry throat. But I spoke it and heard it. Only my sight had been affected.

I heard the rustling again and managed to turn my pounding head slightly. What I saw made my heart begin to pound as well. It was like my nightmare again. Part of the darkness gathered itself into a shape, two shapes, coming toward me. I was helpless. It would do no good to yell, even if I could. I closed my eyes tight and waited.

Something touched my cheek. It was cool and wet and smelled like a leaf. A cool drop fell on my lips. I licked them. It was water. I let my lips open, and the drops of cool water fell into my mouth. I opened my eyes again, but saw only blackness. I could sense that someone knelt over me dropping water into my mouth from something that smelled green, like grass or a leaf. I could sense too that someone else was behind the one giving me water, some-one perhaps only watching, but I began to feel the pres-ence of the second person even more than that of the water giver. Gradually my eyelids grew heavy. I thought, I must be in a hospital. The nurse gives me water, and the doctor stands behind, watching.

But just before I drifted off into a dreamless sleep, I smelled the leaf again and I heard a low, musical chanting from the figure behind. I opened my mouth to ask—and received another drop of cold liquid, this one sweet and aromatic, like rosemary. Then I slept.

I don't know how long I lay this way. The darkness remained. There was no day or night. I slept. I awoke to pain and thirst and was given water and perhaps an herb or drug. Sometimes there was only one person with me, the water-giver kneeling over me. Sometimes the second one came and I waited for the soft, almost unheard chanting that threaded its way into my sleep. I seemed to hang between two dark places, the nightmare of my death-sleep and this waking to blackness and shadows out of my sleep.

Then I awoke with my head clear and cool. I raised it and felt only a slight twinge. And I realized I was hungry. I said, "I'm hungry," into the darkness. I felt the presence of someone leaning over me and I smelled the leaf. I opened my mouth to the drops of water. Then I raised my head again and said, "I'm hungry."

There was a slight pause, a hesitation. Then I felt something touch my lips. It was a finger. It smeared something on my lips. I licked them and tasted a sweet, fruity pulp, like some kind of mush mixed with honey and fruit. The finger continued to dip into something I could not see and carry the sweet substance to my mouth. I licked it off and very shortly felt satisfied. I felt myself being watched. After waiting for a few minutes the figure withdrew.

I waited. Soon it returned with the second shadow. This time the second one came close, and I felt myself being touched, listened to, even smelled. Then both withdrew, and this time I waited for a long time.

I was wide awake. I knew that I had come through something. I'd been close to death, but I was going to live now. I still hurt all over, but the pains were aching and smarting, no longer like stabs deep into me. I still did not dare to move my right leg, and when I touched my head I felt my hair matted in dried blood. But I was going to live. I wondered if I would always be blind. I wondered where I was.

Then I heard them coming back. One, then the other. More. There were more, crowded against one another, so that I knew we must be in a very small place, a place that smelled of earth and grass. They came close and surrounded me, shadows in the dark, like the nightmare again. But this time I was not frightened. I was wide awake and curious.

One of them spoke, not more than three syllables. The sounds made no sense to me, but as he spoke I felt myself moving. They had grasped the mat underneath me, and using it as a stretcher, were half-lifting, half-dragging me, as they moved on their knees. "My leg," I said. "Watch my leg." We moved only a few feet and then came to a narrow, low place where they could not even kneel. Some went ahead and dragged me upward through the narrow place. It was like a short tunnel, not more than eight feet long.

Then suddenly a ray of light hit my eyes like hot sparks. Someone threw something over my eyes, a leaf. Through the veins of the leaf I could see light. "I'm not blind, for Christ's sake, you had me in some God damned cave. Why didn't you . . . "

We were already at the end of the little tunnel. The light had hit my eyes when they threw back the mat that covered the opening.

When they got me outside, they stopped again and knelt down beside me. Someone threw a soft covering over me. They all seemed to be waiting. I was breathing heavily. My leg had hurt quite a bit when they moved me, and the shock of the light had really shaken me. They were giving me a chance to rest.

"Okay, okay, I'm all right," I said.

After another pause someone touched the thing over my eyes. "Yeah, take it off, it's okay," I said. Then while they hesitated I reached up and pulled it off my eyes.

I looked into the face of a boy, a broad fair face with the slight down of a blonde beard. His hair was thick and long, curling down to his shoulders. His face was broad, with high cheek bones, and his eyes were wide and slanted with an oriental fold. He was leaning over me, shielding my face from the sun, so that the sun shone behind his head, lighting up his hair like a halo. I raised my head and looked around. There were five others on their knees facing me. They nodded their heads at me. Then they stood up and picked up the mat again. This time the pain in my leg was worse. My head fell back and I groaned, looking at the sky as we moved.

Now that no one was shading my eyes, the brightness of the sun hurt them. I squinted, and tried to keep my leg still, and I looked around to see where I was. "Do you guys speak English?" The blonde boy turned to me and gave a shrug. I was aware of passing people who stood looking. A naked, brown child ran alongside looking into my face. Then my leg must have been jolted, and the pain shot through me, knocking me out.

The next time I woke up I was alone. I was lying in some kind of tent shaped like a dome. Above me I could see a framework of wooden branches and over them a covering that looked like woven grass, like the mat I was lying on. The dome was about twenty feet in diameter, and contained nothing but some kind of rough blankets hanging from the framework. Near the ground the tent covering was loose, a series of woven mats hanging in separate flaps. One of these flaps had been pulled back, letting in some light. Light came through cracks in the mats above too. The floor was hard dirt covered with some kind of fern. Otherwise the place was bare, cool and quiet, permeated with the smell of the leaf from which I'd sipped water.

I propped myself up on my elbow. My head ached only slightly. I was naked, lying on another woven mat. It felt sticky. Between my body and the mat someone had stuck some wet leaves, and wet leaves were stuck to various parts of my body. I lifted one of them and found a bad gash, which started bleeding when I moved the leaf. I pressed it back into place. Around my leg, grass had been woven in a lacey, stiff stocking.

Beside me on the ground was a light blanket, a pile of fruit that looked like some kind of green plum, and a broad leaf with a pink, pasty substance on it. I dipped my finger into the paste and tasted it; it was the same as what I'd licked off the boy's finger in the dark.

I ate everything, including the leaf, which was tender

like lettuce. Then I covered myself with the blanket and waited for someone to show up. As I waited I speculated on where I might be. I could imagine only two possibilities. One was that my car might have been found by some Indians who took me to their reservation. But I didn't know of any Indian reservation nearby. Besides, the blonde boy didn't look like an Indian. The other possibility, which made more sense, was that I'd fallen into some kind of rural commune. I'd heard about these places, these back-to-nature people going out into the country and growing food and living out of doors. They shunned publicity so there might be a group living quite close by without my knowing it.

But neither explanation dealt with the fact that they didn't seem to speak or understand English.

I was thinking about this when the opening darkened and someone came in, a woman. She was black, not just brown but almost a true black, and tall, with coarse brown hair in a long braid that fell over one shoulder. She wore a colorless tunic that hung to her knees. I remembered that the men who had carried me wore the same thing. As she walked toward me, smiling, I saw she had sharp, pointed features, a long nose, a long face with a pointed chin. She was thin, but hard and muscular; I could see the shape of the muscles in her black arms and legs. She knelt down beside me. Her eyes were blue. "Do you speak English?" I asked.

She shook her head and smiled. Something fluttered on her shoulder beside the braid. It was a white butterfly. I pointed to it, and she nodded and smiled again.

Then I saw she held something in her hand. At first I thought it was a small cup. Then I saw it was made of leaves, folded and woven over one another to form a cup. She took another leaf, dipped it into the leaf cup, then held it to my mouth. It was a kind of warm gruel, like barley. I let her feed me, and when I finished eating, she held the leaf up as if offering it to me. I put it into my mouth and started chewing, and she smiled. She offered me the leaf cup too, and I ate that. She got up.

"Don't go. Sit down here. Let's get acquainted. I want to . . . " But she paid no attention to me. Giving a slight nod of her head to me, she crossed the floor to the opening and went out.

A few minutes later, the boy with golden hair came back, followed by a small yellow dog. He had a handful of wet leaves and he changed some of the ones on my cuts and scratches. Then he sat down on the floor a few feet away from me. The dog sat down next to him and fell asleep.

"You can't speak English," I said, just to be sure. He smiled at me and shrugged.

He stayed until late afternoon, when the glow coming through the opening between the wall mats turned red, then faded into gray. Then he left me. I was alone for several hours as it got dark.

Then he came back. He carried a bowl that looked as if it had been hollowed out from wood. He held it out to me, then reached toward his penis, holding the bowl up. I rolled over on my side and managed to piss into the bowl without spilling much. He picked up the bowl and left.

As soon as he was gone, a whole troop of them marched in, as though they had been waiting for me to finish. I recognized the black woman by her height and the way she moved. But there was not enough moonlight or starlight coming through the opening to make out the others. I counted eleven figures, one of them very small.

They filed in one by one, walking very erect, almost ceremoniously, as if in a formal procession. Each of them went to the wall and took one of the blankets that were hanging there. Two of them helped the little one wrap itself and lie down. Then each one did the same, lying down under the place where his or her blanket had hung, head near the wall, feet pointing toward the center of the tent, like the spokes of a wheel. Then they all murmured something; the sound whispered softly around me. It was the first word of their language I learned, and, as I was to know later, the most important.

"Nagdeo," they said. "Nagdeo, nagdeo," echoed softly until it died into the darkness and I heard only their breathing.

I sat up to try to get one more look at them, and as I squinted through the darkness I saw that I too had been placed as one of the twelve spokes of their wheel, with my feet pointing toward the center of the tent. I lay back and slept.

The pain in my leg woke me while it was still dark. I could see a few stars through an opening between the mats above my head. I watched the sky slowly fade. At the first graying of dawn they began to move.

The first was an old bald man, perhaps in his late fifties. His skin was brown and his legs spindly. But he looked vigorous and strong. I recognized him as one of the men who'd carried me out of the cave. He took off his blanket and hung it on one of the supports of the tent. By that time the black woman was up too.

"Nagdeo."

"Nagdeo."

The two of them stood facing each other. Then they reached their arms upward as if to pull something from the roof. Instead, they swung their arms outward to the side and stood that way for a few seconds. Then, slowly, in simultaneous motion, they brought their hands together prayer-fashion, in front of their chests.

As they stood that way, the bald man began to talk. I recognized his voice. It was the one that had chanted over me in the dark.

This time he did not chant. He seemed to be telling something, conversationally. But this was not a conversation. The black woman stood attentive, listening. His voice trailed on softly. As he spoke a black bird flew in between the mats on the sides of the tent. It flew straight to him and perched on his shoulder. After a while he stopped talking.

There was a slight pause before the black woman started. She spoke for only a few minutes, and he listened just as attentively and silently until she finished. Then they nodded at each other, dropped their hands to their sides, and walked out of the tent. I heard the soft splash of water outside. They were washing.

Gradually the others rose in the same way and went through the same ritual. There were a boy and girl in their teens who grinned at each other throughout the whole thing, and when they were finished kissed each other and held hands on the way out to wash up. The girl was the first I'd seen who looked distinctly Indian, with a broad face and thick coarse hair. But the boy looked almost Greek, like one of the old statues I'd seen in museums,

15

except that his hair was kinky and red. The golden-haired boy went through the ritual with a child who couldn't have been more than three, and who yawned and sucked its thumb the whole time. Then the child mumbled, and the boy listened as attentively as if he were hearing the most important thing that had ever been told him.

I watched a huge man get up. He must have been nearly seven feet tall and built thickly. His head was a mass of bushy black hair and his eyes were almost covered by bushy eyebrows. He made his little speech in a gutteral voice to a bony creature whose sex I couldn't make out. He or she was so old as to be almost hairless, and so skinny that no body contours showed.

Another one, even older, mumbled to a woman with a white kitten perched on her shoulder. She was about the same age as the man with the black bird, the one who had chanted at me. He came back into the tent as she spoke. And, when she had finished, he took her hand and they left the tent together with the cat and the bird eyeing each other from the shoulders on which they rode.

Then a naked boy of about seven (at first I thought it was a girl because of the long hair, until he came close enough for me to see his sex) went through the whole thing with me, chattering as he stood with his hands clasped in front of me. When he was through he looked at me and waited. I shrugged and said, "I don't speak your language." He stood for a few seconds waiting. Then he dropped his hands, gave me a little nod, and walked away. I saw the bushy-haired man pat him on the head and smile.

Within a few minutes they were all gone. As soon as all were out, the golden-haired boy came back in to take care of my toilet needs. And then the black woman came in with a cup of water and a grass tray of fruit. This time she wore a black and orange butterfly.

Then they left me for the rest of the day. The seven year old boy came back several times and just stood there looking at me, then ran off. Once when he saw that I'd eaten all the food, he ran away and came back with the oldest one, who brought another tray of food. I suppose the seven year old had been assigned to keep an eye on me and let them know if I needed anything.

After a couple of weeks of this, I'd have climbed the walls, if I hadn't been sure that I'd bring the whole tent down on me. I'd never been so completely bored. I'd never spent so much time alone. I started dragging myself around the tent. I dragged myself to the opening and looked out, but I couldn't see anything but a low stone wall. Besides, I was naked except for the blanket, and that kept me from going far. I kept the blanket off most of the time because it was a little rough on my healing skin. It too, of course, was woven from grassy fibers.

The people in the tent seemed to take turns caring for me. Except for the early morning ritual, they didn't talk much but they seemed to understand my needs. After I crawled to the doorway, the black woman brought me one of the tunics they wore. It was woven from a softer grass fiber. Actually it was a long strip with a hole in the center, which fit over the head. Then the tunic was wrapped around the body, front over back, and tied around the waist with a braided cord. I put that on, and in the morning, after they had all left the tent, I dragged myself to the doorway and sat there in the sun.

I could see the sky, some other dome-tents, and a series of low stone walls, about three feet high, with trees and ivy growing among them. People like the ones in my tent passed by on their way somewhere, occasionally hopping over the stone walls but more often walking along the paths between them and the tents. As these people passed they nodded to me and sometimes uttered the greeting, "Nagdeo," but mostly they were silent.

At sunset there was a great stream of people passing before me. I decided that the whole village must pass by at that time, all going somewhere, probably to eat. There were always fruit and leaves lying around among shells and water pots perched on the low stone walls, but I never saw any adults eating. I assumed (correctly) that they must eat somewhere else and that the fruit was left there for children or anyone else who couldn't wait until sundown for a meal.

I counted them several times as they passed by, and knew there must be fewer than one hundred and fifty including babies carried in arms. They all dressed alike and all walked alike: silent, erect and somehow tensed, as if listening to something. They reminded me of the look I'd seen on the faces of people who carry transistor radios around and listen to them all day long—that faraway, attentive look. The younger ones ran or skipped, but even they seemed occasionally to be skipping in time to music only they could hear.

Most of the people were of a racial blend I could not quite identify. They were of medium height and build and all, of course, sun-tan or brown. Their features formed a medium composite: eyes neither narrow nor round, noses neither flat nor pointed, lips neither full nor thin. Their hair varied from the lightest and finest to the darkest or coarsest.

But a large minority of them had startling combinations of physical traits, like the black woman with the nordic features and blue eyes, or the golden-haired boy with oriental eyes, like signs of recent interbreeding, or mutations, or throw-backs. I saw no sign that these extreme types were in any way noticed or thought of as different by the others.

Yet at first I completely missed these dramatic differences and thought of the people as looking all alike. I was used to superficial conventions of clothing, grooming and manner. I had become so blinded to people's real faces and bodies that, when I watched these people walk by, I was often unsure even of their sex.

Since all wore their hair long and all wore the same shapeless, kneelength tunic, only beards and body contour were definite signs. Up to the age of sexual maturity the children were naked and long-hared and unless I made a special point of looking for a little penis, they were sexless to me, or all rather like little girls because of their long hair. The old people looked alike in their own way, as, without special clothes and make-up, old men and women do tend to look sexlessly alike, the women growing some facial hair, the men's features softening, bodies getting skinny and shapeless.

But even in the middle age range I was occasionally confused beause of the total lack of sexual roles. The men waited on me as often as the women did, and on each other. The tent was cleaned out every few days, the fern branches shaken out, the floor tamped and brushed, but everyone helped with the work. I saw no difference of

19

function, except the women obviously nursed the infants; but the men carried and cared for the small ones as much as the women did.

I made the mistake of thinking that there were many more babies and children than there actually were. Each time I saw a man or woman carrying a baby or holding the hand of a child, I connected the child with the adult. But gradually I began to recognize the little ones. There were not very many, and it was hard to tell who their parents were. They seemed to be passed from one to another. I learned finally who the mothers were, as the babies were passed back to the same women to be nursed. But I hardly noticed the babies anyway. They were inconspicuous because they were quiet. During the whole time I was there I never heard a baby cry, except for the first, aggrieved cry of birth.

Many of the people were accompanied by pet animals or birds. The black woman had a different colored butterfly riding on her shoulder every day and the bald man was seldom without the black bird perched as if sprouting from his shoulder. The white cat seemed to stare suspiciously at me over the shoulder of the woman who was always with him. The golden-haired boy had his yellow dog, which was always curling up to sleep. The bushy-haired giant was incongruously following by a bleating lamb. And one five or six year old girl made me a bit nervous every time she walked past with her six foot green snake circling her shoulders.

I don't mean to give the impression that I was observing the people and learning about them at this stage. What I learned came to me in spite of myself, for I had nothing but the slightest curiosity about them.

I was far too absorbed in my own problems. All day I lay around watching my wounds heal, waiting for my bruises and my pains to fade, wiggling my leg tentatively as the grass stocking softened and disintegrated. If I sat alert in the opening of the tent, it was only because I expected at any time to see the local police come down the path to drive me back to town. I knew I had to get well and strong so as to get away, but I could not imagine where to go.

I devised plan after plan.

I would call my agent for some money and would take off for Mexico.

I would go back to face the mess, call my lawyer and maybe get off with probation or at most a couple of years in prison.

I would deny the whole thing, say I'd gone on a trip and Connie had been killed by a burglar. I would just call someone as soon as I got off the reservation and be surprised and grieved. I would call Connie's number first of all. That was a clever touch. It might work.

It never occurred to me to think of staying there for any length of time. That's why I made no attempt to learn the language and had little interest in the customs or the people. I had, I thought, enough to think about.

One night I had a strange dream. I was in a doctor's office having my leg examined. The doctor was dressed in surgical clothes, mask and all. He took the grass cast off my leg, examined the leg, and then led me to an enormous and complicated piece of machinery. It loomed over me, threateningly. He told me to put my leg under it. I was afraid. Then he said that if I wanted my leg to heal more quickly I should submit it to the machine. Otherwise it would heal, of course, but very slowly. He seemed not to care one way or the other, but simply stood waiting for me to decide. Finally I put my leg straight out, under the huge mechanism. The doctor pulled a switch. The machine lit up—and then out of it came the chanting sound I'd heard in the cave. The sound continued for some minutes. Then it stopped and the doctor switched off the machine. "Stand up and walk," he said. And I did.

The morning after that dream, it happened that the bald man who'd done the chanting chose to go through the ritual with me. I waited until he was through talking. Then as he let his arms fall to his sides, I pointed to my leg.

"How about it, old witch doctor?" I said. "Can you have me dancing by noon?"

I caught a look in his eye that showed me he understood my tone if not my words. He turned away.

"Wait a minute. I'm serious." He turned back. "I really am," I said. I pointed to my leg again. "Anything that will get me on my feet sooner."

He left and came back a few minutes later with a stick. He made motions as if to use it as a crutch. I nodded and took the stick. "But is that the best you can do?" I guess my disappointment was evident.

He looked at me doubtfully for a moment, then (somewhat reluctantly, I thought) went outside and got the other people of our tent. They went down on their knees in a circle around me. The old man chanted for a minute, then reached forward and touched my leg. That was all. It was all over. Everyone got up, and two of the men—the big bushy-haired one and the boy I'd started to call goldy-locks—helped me to my feet. The bald man handed me the stick again and gave me an abrupt nod.

All day, while they were gone, I practiced hobbling around on the stick. That night they repeated the little chanting circle. I slept very deeply afterward and the next morning was able to pull myself up on the stick without any help. That day I hobbled around the paths outside the tent. By the time the circle gathered that night again, I was very eager. This time I closed my eyes and clasped my hands the way the others in the circle did, and concentrated on the chant.

When I woke up the next morning, I could stand without the stick.

And I went into complete panic. For now I had to do something. So long as I was hurt and sick, it was plausible that I should remain here without attempting to communicate with the nearest town. But as soon as I was on my feet there was no reason not to—unless I had reason to hide.

My disappearance must have been noted soon after Connie's death. Sooner or later the wreckage of my car would be found. Sooner or later someone would come here from the nearest town and would notice me, or the authorities would routinely search the place. They often raided such communes first of all, expecting to find fugitives there. I was surprised no one had come yet. Maybe tomorrow someone would. Or the next day.

I had to move before they did. And I could not.

I understand now the state that I was in then. It was a part of all that I had made of myself. It was a part of my success.

And I was a success, in every way that I could wish. I

was that rare man: a man who had gotten everything he wanted.

I had shown my writing talent early, while I was still in high school. I won prizes. My talent was combined with a flair for taking tests: that quick, superficial ability to out-guess the pedantry of mechanized stupidity, that passes for intelligence. It got me scholarships to good colleges. Of course, I edited the school paper and the literary magazine and I published my own poetry before graduation.

Even so, I easily saw that, regardless of my talents, degrees without contacts would get me nothing but the starvation of a serious writer or the dull security of teaching.

I got a job in a quiet, exclusive girls' college where I could write more poetry, spill a few words of wisdom to the panting adolescents and rise in the respect of my literary colleagues while I waited to meet the rich young student I would marry. The young things fell into my bed like cut grass. I could have chosen among three or four that first year; they were all so eager to break their parents' hearts by marrying a defiant, arrogant academic opportunist. I chose the most staunchly rebellious one and we eloped.

Now I could live without working, pretending to write poetry while looking down my nose at her family, who hastened to support us. But the money was not enough, a small gain, really, for a man with an appetite like mine.

I wanted something . . . something I couldn't define. Something like the first thrill that comes with a first winning—a first publication of your work, a first good job, a first good lay, a first . . . all the orgasms of life, that while you're having them make you think, "this is it . . . this is the great thing, now that I've got this, I've made it." But almost before you've finished saying it, you're on your way down, the thrill is waning, the orgasm is over and you can't reach it quite that way again. But you keep trying to duplicate it, you try all the variations, to get there, before you exhaust that way and begin to try some other. That was what my life was really all about; the lower I sank, the higher I was trying to reach, trying to live life on that orgasmic plane, clutching and trying to hang on, falling and trying to get back.

The world is full of ways to try to reach it. Drugs and drink and sex and fame and things . . . plenty of things. You can spend years, from your first shiny tricycle to your last taste of power, and take a long, long time before you know finally, fully, before you realize that you always come down, no matter how high you've been; that it's a law of gravity of the soul.

That's when a lot of people commit suicide, when they stop believing it's possible to live really alive, when their own weight becomes too much for them.

But I was a long way from that, or thought I was. I lived off my wife's money while I concocted a novel of obscene urbanity: a spy story with a ruthless, indestructible hero and equal parts of sex and violence. Among my father-in-law's contacts was a publisher who owed him a favor. (The university presses which had published my poetry wouldn't touch it, of course.)

I hit it just right. Some people read it for the sex, some for the violence, some because others were reading it. It crossed all intellectual lines, the low brows identifying with the hero, the high-brows pretending they found it all very funny. When the book hit the top of the best seller lists, I left my wife.

I turned out four more of them, released them one a year, signed film contracts, and at thirty was rich and famous. I even looked like the hero of the books, lean and hard, for in the effort I'd increasingly lost weight and had what Connie and the others, all those others, called a hungry look. There was even some talk of using me to act the role for the movies. I'd already done some introductions for a TV mystery series and any number of frustrated people had adopted my face as the face of their fantasy identity or fantasy lover.

It was all fine, except for the nightmares. And the nightmares were, perhaps, the only real thing in my life.

I knew all the rest was phony. I knew my popularity would wane, but not before I'd made a lot of money and would then be able to . . . able to what? I hadn't thought of the next stage, the next orgasm, yet. But I was coming down.

The nightmares were more frequent. And women—women like Connie—sometimes became absolutely savage, as though being with me turned them into some kind of screeching witches.

But I was a success, I told myself. I was what all men wanted to be, God help them.

I hardly left the tent that day, not even to stand in the opening. I rehearsed my story. I had decided to try the trip story: I'd gone away for a rest, telling Connie she could use the house while I was gone. I'd had an accident. As soon as I was able I'd gone back to town. I hadn't seen a newspaper, so I had no way of knowing what had happened. No, I had no idea who could have done it. Of course, Connie was a woman who got around—there were any number of men, perhaps a jealous lover or ex-husband . . . she had two of them.

As I paced round and round the tent with only a slight limp, the story sounded more and more plausible. After all, if I couldn't dream up a good story, who could?

The sky was turning a deep gold, and I heard footsteps. I went to the opening, pulled back the mat, and stepped outside. The people were coming down the path in their daily sunset procession. Today they seemed to be livelier than usual. Some of the younger ones were holding hands and moving in a kind of skipping, hopping dance along the path. One of them missed a step, and the others laughed and embraced him. Then he laughed, and they stretched out their arms, held hands and moved forward again. As they passed by me, they pointed to my leg, gave a high kick, a laugh, and skipped onward.

As other people passed by they gave me a similar greeting or congratulations on being on my feet. From some the greeting was a simple nod, from others, like the bushy-haired giant, it was a robust shake of his clasped hands, like the gesture of a winning prize fighter (followed by an ironic bleat from his trailing lamb). I felt like an important dignitary before whom all the people were passing in review.

As they passed some picked up sea shells which sat on top of the wall. I learned later that these were used for eating and drinking. Afterwards they were returned to the stone walls where the sun bleached them clean and where they caught rain water and were available for a drink or a wash.

When the black woman, the bald man, the cat woman and goldy-locks came by they stopped and stood beside me. They seemed to be waiting for everyone else to go. When the path had been empty for a few moments, goldy-locks took my hand and drew me away from the doorway to the center of the path. He put my hand on his shoulder. The black woman came alongside and put my other hand on her shoulder. A green butterfly took off from her shoulder and lit on her ear. The old man and woman went ahead.

We walked in silence for a few steps. Then the woman ahead started chanting. Her white cat eyed me steadily over her shoulder. We walked slowly as if to let me test my leg and lean for support. But there was no problem. Except for a slight weakness the leg was all right.

The path curved. It seemed to curve always to the left. We were walking in a circle, a continuously narrowing circle. Along the path were other tents like the one I'd been in. And I could see our destination, in the center of the narrowing circles marked by the low stone walls.

It was a huge pointed tent, like an Indian tent, built up on a slight rise. This tent was uncovered. The great logs of trees pointed upward and came together in the center but there was little covering, no matted roof.

We came around one more turn and the low stone wall ended at a wide, clear pool with stones lining its edges. The old man and woman went to the edge of the pool, scooped up water in their hands, and washed their hands and faces, taking care to spill the water over the plants growing round the pool, not actually washing themselves in the pool. After washing they scooped a few drops of clear water into their hands and carried it forward. The three of us followed their example.

Beyond the pool the path now led up the rise toward the huge, skeletal tent. As we climbed upward I leaned more heavily on the boy and the woman. The old man and woman went on ahead, both of them chanting, as though they had forgotten us.

I stumbled over something and looked down. It was a tree root. The black woman sprinkled her little handful of water over the exposed root. The others were doing the same, sprinkling their few drops of water on the exposed roots or the ground around a great old tree that now stood before us.

I had never seen a tree like it. Its roots had spread out for yards beyond the path, and its trunk filled the path, which was at least eight feet wide. Its bark was nearly black and deeply rutted and gnarled. Starting from a height of above five feet, branches twisted outward like a roof, then curved upward. The leaves were broad and thick, a dark bluish-green with red veins running through them.

We had to duck under and go around the tree. It was quite dark under the thick branches. We climbed carefully over the roots, until we reached the other side, the entrance to the tent.

I stopped short and looked down. The mound on which the tent was built had been hollowed out and steps cut into the side, like a broad, shallow, inverted cone going down into the earth to a central point which glowed with a red flame. Seated on the steps along the sides of the cone were the entire population and a sizable number of animals. They were in complete silence, looking deep down into the flaming center of the cone. Then, as if at a signal, they stood up, lifted their heads, and gazed upward to where the tree trunk poles of the tent joined high above them.

As they stood this way, several boys and girls turned and came toward us. They lifted me onto their shoulders and began walking down the steps. The old man and woman continued ahead of us and the black woman and goldy-locks followed behind. I started to object, but in the complete stillness my voice sounded so strange that it startled even me before it died off.

People stood at random on the steps. There was no straight pathway down. The boys and girls carried me around and among the people going step by step. All the people, even the children, kept their eyes upward, fixed on the joined beams of the great tent. Again and again I followed their gaze, and as we descended deeper into the cone, the massive logs above seemed to pierce more deeply upward into the sky where they converged in the center.

For one ridiculous, panic-stricken second I believed that they were going to carry me to the deepest center of the cone and throw me into the flames. At that point one of the children cheated; looking away from the tent-top, he sneaked a quick look at me. When he caught my eye he grinned and stopped me from making a fool of myself. I'd been about to start screaming and thrashing.

The fire in the center was set in a great pit. Earthen pots sat around the edges. The boys and girls circled the flames with me three times and then set me down.

The bald man and cat woman began to chant again, but this time the chant was taken up by the boys and girls. The nearest people joined in, and then others beyond them, and beyond them. As they joined in the chant they lowered their gaze from the tent-top and looked down at me.

I call it a chant, but it was not really that. It was a wordless song beginning with the thread of melody from the old woman and woven round and round by the others as they joined. The harmonies thickened, becoming tightly complex, then suddenly opened out, like the unraveling of knotted threads. The melody moved to higher and higher pitches, the harmonies thickening at each rise, until suddenly all the voices landed on a high note of unison that pierced like a bright light. Then silence.

The silence lasted for only a moment. Then somebody giggled. The boys and girls who had carried me ran up the steps again. The first row of people stepped forward toward me, but then went beyond me to the fire. They picked up some of the earthen posts and went up the steps. One of them came to me, pulled something out of a pot and held it up to my mouth. I opened my mouth, and he put it in. It tasted like sweet potato.

Everyone around me was laughing and smiling. People carried pots and walked around putting bits of food in the mouths of others. No one fed himself from the pots, except one or two of the small children. I noticed that when they fed themselves, someone always rushed up to them, smiling, and fed them from another pot. Then someone would take the pot away from the child and feed him and others, unless the child caught on fast enough to start feeding others.

The black woman walked up to me and held out a morsel, smiling at me. I took it in my mouth and looked straight into her blue eyes as I chewed and swallowed. Then I took the pot from her and, never dropping my gaze from hers, I took a bit of the food in my fingers and offered it to her. She smiled and opened her mouth. I reached for more, but she made a gesture toward the people around her. They were looking at me expectantly as if they wanted me to feed them. When I walked around putting food into their mouths they laughed and clasped their hands and made general gestures of delight. I supposed that they considered it a special honor to be fed by me, until I noticed that they made the same gesture when a small child stopped feeding himself and held out food toward others.

There wasn't much food, and it took a long time to get everyone fed by this inefficient method, but everyone finally seemed to get enough. The people who emptied the pots cleaned them out with leaves, which were also eaten, then put them in a row around the fire.

The fire had died down to coals now, but the place was warm and comfortable. Everyone began to sit down on the steps again. I sat down in the front row next to the black woman. There were some murmurs, but generally everyone was getting quiet, as if they expected something.

When everyone was seated and quiet, the woman with the white cat stepped forward. Somebody put a thick mat on the ground near the fire. She sat down crosslegged on it and began to speak. It was the first time I'd heard anyone talk at length. I couldn't understand a word, and I couldn't identify the language, yet I felt I should be able to.

It reminded me of the time I had tried to practice my high school French on a native speaker, a boy who was visiting the States and could speak no English. What he spoke sounded like French, sounded like something I should understand. The structure of the sentences made sense, but the words did not. I could not understand a thing he said. I learned later that he spoke a provincial dialect.

This was how I felt listening to the woman as she droned on and on. The language was familiar, but I could not understand a word. It was English, yet it was not. It did not sound like any foreign language. The rhythms and word order somehow made sense to me. But I could not understand the words. ·

The red glow from the coals grew dim, and we saw the woman only by starlight. She held up one of the pots near the fire and, still talking, reached into it. Drawing her hand out, she sprinkled some sparkling drops over her head. I blinked, and they were gone. Her voice droned on.

I must have fallen asleep. I felt myself being lifted and I woke up. It was completely dark except for the stars that showed between the tent poles above. They carried me up the steps, out of the cone, down the circular paths and all the way back to the tent. Still groggy, I went inside and lay down, remembering to take my place as a spoke in the wheel-like sleeping arrangement. Then I fell asleep again.

I awoke while it was still dark. All the bodies around me were still. I lay and thought about the experience of the evening.

I had been through a ceremony, perhaps a kind of welcoming ritual. Whoever these people were, they were not an Indian tribe or a group that had fled the city. But who were they, and where was I? Their welcoming ceremony was harmless enough, but it implied that they expected me to stay, and might even keep me here by force.

They had simply not existed for me as real people before. I was concerned only with myself and with the world I had to go back to. But now my attention had been forced to include them and this place. It was time for me to find out something about where I was. Or maybe it was time for me to leave. Maybe I should just walk out, right now.

I got up very quietly, keeping my blanket wound around me. I was near the opening, and only fumbled for a moment in pulling back the flap. Then I was outside on the path.

The night had remained clear. The sky was dead black, with stars piercing brightly. I could see the spokes of the great tent above the trees. In the opposite direction I saw a hill, shining gray in the moonlight. I shook my right leg. Could I make it? The hill was not so very far away, not so very high. I could walk there, climb the hill, by sunrise. From the hill perhaps I would see a road or even possibly a town.

I set off at once, keeping my eyes on the hill. Rather than following the paths, I went straight, stepping over the low stone walls of the paths, passing by other tents like the one I stayed in. All was very still except that along the way I disturbed the animals.

A squatty reddish dog sat up as I passed; sheep, goats and rodent-like things shifted restlessly. One large spotted cat followed me for a while. Birds perched everywhere, flapped their wings and cocked one eye at me.

But very soon, by cutting across the paths, I came to the end of the tents. Beyond them I saw rows of strange little mounds. When I got close, they looked like igloos, with low, crawl-in tunnels leading to them. I stopped and looked at one, remembering. It must have been in one of these, not in a cave, that they had put me when they found me.

Beyond the little igloo-mounds were open fields, with earth that was soft. I sank into the soft dirt as I walked, and looking down I could see some kind of small, young growth. I bent down and pulled up a leaf. It was the kind I had eaten, the kind woven into cups, used for spoons, for cleaning out the pots. This must be where they cultivated their food, perhaps working in the fields all day.

Beyond the field I came to rows and rows of small trees. Gradually the trees became thicker and there were more bushes among them. I lost sight of the hill and could only guess at where I was heading. I sat down to rest several times. My leg was very tired.

Then I saw that the ground sloped upward slightly. I knew I had reached the base of the hill, and that thought gave me a new burst of energy. I pushed upward, panting as the climb became steeper and steeper. The hill was higher than I thought, but that only meant I would see more when I got to the top. The sky was fading. Before long, the sun would rise, and at about that time I would reach the top of the hill. It was easier now because I could see better. The trees were thinning out, and the ground was quite light.

I began to feel the warmth of the rising sun on my back. The ground was grassy now. The top of the hill I could see ahead of me, a grassy plain from which I could be able to look in all directions. The sky beyond it was pale blue now. And I had gotten my second wind. I hardly panted at all as I gave the last pull upward that landed me on the edge of a meadow on the top of the hill.

The first thing I saw was the face of a small brown goat that stood looking intently at me, as if it had been expecting me. It watched me for a moment, then in quick leaps crossed the meadow and disappeared.

I turned around and looked toward the horizon behind me. And I felt my breath knocked out of me as no climb could have done. I looked to my left, to my right. I ran—as well as I could stumblingly, limpingly run—across the meadow toward the west and looked. I rubbed my eyes.

Then I walked along the edge of the meadow, circling the entire, flat top of the hill, scanning the horizon in every direction.

When I came back to the point where I had started, I sat down in the grass, sat very still, waiting for the reality of my vision to sink into reality in my mind.

On the horizon, as far as I could see, in every direction, was water. I was on an island.

Two

From where I sat I could look straight down upon the village. At the center of it was the great tent, rising above the huge old tree. The low stone walls started from the tree, spiraling outward in wider and wider circles. Along the wall, at irregular intervals, were tent domes like the one I stayed in. I counted twelve of them. The stone wall ended abruptly at the last one. Then the spiral continued with the little igloo type mounds; there were over twenty of them blending outward irregularly into the fields beyond.

Then suddenly the whole village disappeared. I blinked and it came back. As I focused and unfocused my eyes upon the village it alternately melted into scrubby ground and reappeared in its spiral design, like a shifting optical illusion game or an expert work of camouflage.

Many people were already up. I saw them come out of their tents and move outward from the spiral. Some of them followed the spiraling path, but many simply hopped over the low stone walls. Beyond the outermost stone walls were piles of sticks and bones. People stopped at these piles to pick up a tool and moved outward to the fields where they began to work in irregularly spaced groups. Others came to the very edge of the fields, below me, and worked among the trees in the orchards.

I sat there the whole day, my mind in suspension, but my senses alert. Some people stayed in the fields nearly all day while others went back into the village after only a couple of hours. There was constant coming and going in the little igloos outside the village. I'd have thought they were used as some kind of latrines if I hadn't been in one, and if the people hadn't stayed so long—at least an hour—during each visit to one.

Occasionally I saw a group of workers suddenly stop work and begin to move together in a kind of dance. Sometimes they joined hands in a line, but more often they just faced each other, or faced toward the center of a square or circle, and did slow unison movements, bending far backward, swinging their arms in broad waves, stepping long slow strides. However their movements went, they always stopped the same way: erect, hands at sides, heads thrown back. They would laugh and go back to working in the soil, their work taking on the same rhythmic quality.

Children went among them with a bag that must have contained water. They drank, danced and worked.

When the sun was directly overhead many of them went back to the village. Others lay in the shade of trees or went into the little igloos. In the afternoon many of them were back at work in the fields again. I heard the sound of bees, of birds calling, of the breeze rustling leaves and grass. When the wind was right I could hear the faint gushing of an unseen river, and once in the late afternoon, the wind brought me the echo of the ocean waves on some beach out beyond the hill. Mingled with these sounds were the occasional bursts of laughter or singing from the workers in the fields. But the entire day passed without my hearing from them one spoken word.

As the sun moved low on the horizon, the hill cast its shadow over the fields nearest me, and the people, one by one, began to stop work and move toward the village. On the far side of the village, where the fields circled almost beyond my sight, to the next hill, I saw the people as little dots, moving toward the village.

Then I heard a familiar sound, a rattling drone, a whoshing roar. A plane was passing overhead. I looked up into the sky but I could see nothing. It was flying too high. Already the sound was dying away.

As I looked back down into the valley I saw a frozen scene come back to life. I thought my vision was playing tricks on me, for it seemed that all the people had for a few seconds frozen absolutely in the midst of a movement, like a movie that stops to become a still picture and then is animated again. Now that they were in motion again, I felt doubtful that they had stopped at all.

While they had left the village in various ways, they all now entered it the same way. From the point where the low stone walls began, they walked the spiral inward, in the procession which I had seen daily. They stopped at various tents, then moved onward in the processing leading to the great central tent. As the sky darkened, the fields and village looked empty, and I knew that they were all in the cone under the great spokes of the uncovered tent, eating.

I felt weak and cold. I climbed down the hill, stumbling a couple of times, but not hurting myself. At the foot of the hill I reached into one of the trees and picked some of the small green plums. I ate them on my way across the fields, and immediately felt stronger. It was quite dark as I reached the stone wall, and clouds hid the moon. So I followed closely along the low stone walls, rather than stepping over them, following the slow spiral inward as the others had done before me. Keeping one hand on top of the walls I noticed that they were slightly indented, as if a shallow gutter ran along the top. I imagined that when it rained, the water was caught in those gutters, running inward to fill the pool below the great old tree.

When I reached the end of the stone wall, I could see the waters of the pool glistening. The clouds had passed and the night was clear. I splashed some water on my face. Then I bent under the branches of the great tree and found my way to the great tent, where I stood on the edge looking down into the cone.

This time, in front of the glowing embers of the fire, there were ten or twelve children, naked, going through what looked like some kind of dance. They joined hands, circled the fire, extended their hands toward the fire, raised their right hands high, then extended these hands toward the people sitting on the first step near them. The people stretched out their hands as if to receive something, then turned and stretched out their hands behind them, as if to pass it on. The motion was repeated, step by step, all the way up.

Over and over again, the children moved silently through the dance; the arms of the audience swung forward and backward. After a few minutes I began to feel slightly dizzy at the waves of motion. Then I thought I saw a slight glow in the hands of one of the children. I blinked my eyes, and it was gone. I started to move forward down the steps, but I felt afraid of the mass of waving arms. Finally I decided to stand on the edge of the cone until the ritual ended. Several times I felt giddy. Several times I thought I saw some shining objects passed from hand to hand in the darkness.

The dance ritual didn't really end. It just faded away as one by one the children tired and sat down or lay down or returned to a seat on the steps. The last one held his hand above the fire for a moment, then abruptly sat down. All motion stopped and there was complete silence.

Into that silence, I shouted. "Doesn't anyone here speak English!" All heads turned toward me. My shout sounded so stupid that I expected them to laugh. But no one did. The faces I could see in the semi-darkness looked uncertain, then concerned, then welcoming. Arms reached out to me and led me down the steps. Someone stepped forward to stir up the fire, and it flared into brightness. Then Goldy-locks stepped forward, squinted his slant eyes at me and said, "Chil-sing," then put his fingers to his chest. He repeated this several times, then looked at me and waited.

I touched his chest with one finger and repeated, "Chil-sing." He nodded and smiled. Everyone nodded and smiled. Heads were bobbing all around me. They had understood that I wanted to communicate, and they were teaching me their language, starting with names.

Hopelessly I acquiesced. Certainly I could find out nothing about where I was and what was going to happen to me until I knew how to communicate with them. I pointed to my chest and said my name. There was no response at all. Chil-sing just looked at me. Slowly he shook his head. Everyone else started shaking heads. The motion was eerie repeated in the darkness all around me.

"Idiots. I'm telling you my name."

Chil-sing put his hand on my shoulder and shrugged as if he wanted to change the subject. I pulled my shoulder away from his grasp. He looked stricken. He bowed his head and murmured something that sounded like an apology. Many of the surrounding people did the same. It was exasperating.

"Look," I said. "Let's give up the language lesson for tonight. I'm tired. We're all tired. Let's go to sleep. Huh? Tired?" I started going through some gestures of sleep, and they finally caught on. People started getting up, but they stood still in their places until one of the old ones stood up before the fire and chanted something, just a phrase or two. Then she said, "Nagdeo, nagdeo, nagdeo." The whole group repeated the word three times and then they started to file out.

Chil-sing and the bald man waited for me. They started to take my arms, but I shrugged them away. They followed me. Once we got past the tree and the pool I started short-cutting, stepping over the stone walls, and they followed me. I lost my way and couldn't find our tent, until one of them nudged me and led the way. Then I stumbled into the tent, rolled up in my blanket and fell dead asleep.

The next morning I was up first. The next one up was the black woman. She stood in front of me, reached up her arms, spread them wide and started to clasp them in front. But I interrupted. I reached forward, pointing to her breast, just short of touching her right nipple, and said "What's your name?" She looked surprised. I pointed again.

"Augustine," she murmured. Then she clasped her hands and began telling me whatever she was telling. I interrupted her, pointed to the framework of the wall and demanded, "What do you call this?"

She paid no attention to me, but finished her incomprehensible recital. Then she looked where I was pointing and said "Ka." I pointed to the mat covering the framework, to the floor, to the opening, and she simply repeated, "Ka."

Then she motioned for me to follow her outside. Others were already on the paths walking outward. No one hopped walls and everyone walked slowly. As they passed trees and bushes they picked a blossom or a twig. I noticed that several butterflies circled the head of the black woman, and one finally lit on her shoulder.

"That's some trick, Augustine," I said. "Will you teach it to me?"

She only smiled.

We walked single file now, out across the fields and onto a trail through a thick forest. Then we came to a river and walked along its banks until, widening and slowing, the river too became silent. The next sound I heard was that of the sea. We walked past a large rocky mound, into the sand, and saw and heard the rushing surf, with the sun rising above it.

I fell on the sand, too exhausted to move. The people filed past me and walked straight toward the water. On the edge of the water they pulled off their tunics and left them on the sand.

They waited, standing on the edge of the sea, until all were there, standing in a straight line along the edge of the water, naked, facing the rising sun. Then each took the leaf or blossom he carried and threw it forward into the water. As their blossoms were carried outward in the receding waves, they joined hands and followed them into the water.

When the water reached waist-height I heard squeals and laughter as they began paddling about, washing themselves and one another. They played like any sea bathers on a Sunday afternoon. And, in fact, I learned later that this was their sabbath, which came about every seven days (depending on the weather and the work) and which always started with an ocean bath, even in cold weather, except during the worst of winter.

They came out of the water one by one, put on their tunics and began to organize games and dances on the sand. These went on until the sun was high. Then we started back.

I was too tired to make it all the way. Before we reached the fields, the bushy-haired man swooped me up in his arms, as if I were a baby. "Sbgai," he identified himself as we jogged along. And that was how we entered the village, leading the procession, his little lamb bleating behind us.

The rest of the day was spent sitting around the village. Small circles formed around single people, usually old ones, who recited long monologues. I joined one group with Sbgai. Every now and then I would catch a word, repeat it to Sbgai and challenge him to translate it. By the end of the day I had learned about twenty words, was more confused than before, and only slightly less bored.

There is no point in detailing the process of my lauguage lessons. I followed people around throughout the next few days, pointing to things and asking their names.

I have always been quick with languages, easily picking up a working knowledge of several. After a few days I concluded that, judging from their language these people were so backward as to be a race of mental retardants. The vocabulary I heard was small and general. I understood that ka meant dwelling place or tent, but all parts of the ka were simply referred to as ka. Similarly there was a word for food, and anything edible was called by that word, with no differentiation. All trees, bushes, plants- —anything that grew—had one name. All stones, of whatever color or type, had one name. All animals had one name—even birds and insects were included in it. And the same word (which was only a slightly elongated form of the word for plants) meant people too. I couldn't see how they could communicate anything at all with a language of such poverty.

And, of course, they didn't communicate much with words. They seemed to try to avoid speaking as much as possible, using gestures when they needed to tell someone something. This hampered me a great deal because although they would speak when I demanded to know a word, would answer any question I asked, it was really impossible to engage them in conversation.

The younger ones were less taciturn. I began to spend a lot of time with Chil-sing and some of the children. In fact, I developed quite a following. They were willing to talk, and I got them to the point where they would chatter for minutes at a time until some adult came and quietly led them away.

That made me believe that the older ones were trying to hide something from me. For all their smiling and all their care of me, they were holding back, I felt sure of it. Otherwise, why would they take the children away after they had talked to me for a while? What were they afraid the children would tell me?

In a few weeks I knew all of the poor vocabulary they used every day, but I could still not understand much of what they said upon awakening in the morning nor much of what was said around the fire in the la-ka (the big tent) at night. I only caught a word here and there in these long speeches, which contained a large vocabulary of words saved up, as it were, for the occasion.

I intently watched and listened every night in the la-ka. I felt that it was here, in the long monologue, that I would learn the subtleties of their language, if any existed. But more than that I was intrigued with what I saw.

The second time the children acted out their little fire drama or dance, I watched more closely, and this time I was sure that what they passed from hand to hand were rubies.

Another children's drama took place to spoken words, a chant—the first of the stories told in the la-ka whose words I was able to understand. It was simple enough:

We seek
All seek
Where? Where?

As the chant was repeated a child danced up and down the steps, making motions as if she were hunting for something among the people, while the other children stood behind the fire chanting. When the child reached the top step, the chanters shouted, "There! Where? In you!"

I looked up to see the child's mouth open wide with joy—and between her teeth I saw a pearl as big as an egg. Then, some quick sleight of hand, and it was gone.

That night, as we left the la-ka, I stopped Augustine and said, "You live a very hard, simple life by day, but at night you display your treasures in the la-ka." She smiled and nodded. "Is there more than I have seen?"

She turned to face me. This time she did not smile. "Much more."

I could not read her expression. I decided that these people were a mixture of subtlety and stupidity. They obviously knew the value of the precious gems I had glimpsed, and they prized them, but only as a decoration to their stories and rituals, not as a means for improving their material condition. Could it be possible that they did not know the monetary value of them? That seemed unlikely, yet I saw no sign, so far, that they had any contact or had ever had any contact with my world. I suspected them of trying to avoid contact, of hiding their existence. Why? To keep from having their treasure stolen? Yet, without contact with the outside world how could they know that anyone would want to steal the precious stones?

I saw no sign of any mining on the island. When I asked where the precious stones came from, I was greeted with blank stares. Communication was still difficult, and I gave up in frustration at their ignorance or reticence, whichever it might be. Whatever they were hiding, I felt sure I would find out before long from such simple people.

I remember thinking, at that time, that it was appropriate they should call themselves by the same word they gave to animals. They seemed hardly more than animals in their simplicity and lack of human consciousness.

As I went on learning the language I ran into several difficulties. Their verbs lacked tense—literally, as they spoke, there was no sense of past or future, only of now, the present moment. That's why it would be impossible, if not boring, but surely confusing for my reader if I tried to translate directly any talks I had with them. And the reader must understand that, as I report future talks, when I knew the language better, I must distort these talks to fit a language into which what they said really cannot be translated.

The language lacked all sense of the singular, the individual. But what most struck me, next to the lack of a sense of time, was its inconsistency of gender. Everything animate and inanimate was either masculine or feminine, nothing was neuter—except human beings. I'd never encountered anything like this in any other language.

And it was no accident, but a reflection of the way they lived. Great care was taken to pair "masculine" and "feminine" objects in planting or arranging things. I would have said that no people could be more constantly concerned with sex. Yet I never heard anyone referred to by pronouns of gender—no he or she. There were words for man and woman but they were almost never used.

I have already mentioned similarity of work between the sexes and similarity of clothing. Ornaments too were worn by both sexes. There seemed to be only one consistent rule or custom about ornaments. People might put a flower or a woven necklace on someone else, then stand back to enjoy the effect. But I never saw anyone decorate himself or herself, or show any sign of concern for appearance. Ornaments, like food, were to be given to others.

One pronoun referred to all human beings. People called to one another by this word when not using someone's name, or they referred to one or more people by it. It was both singular and plural and it meant kinship. The way most people use the word "brother" would be the closest word in English, but because "brother" implies gender and singularity, it is quite wrong. The closest word I can think of to approximate the meaning of this pronoun is "kin." We were all called kin.

But as soon as I started feeling better, I had something else besides language on my mind. I remember thinking at the time that every island paradise in the books I'd read or written (one of the spy stories actually did take place partially on a South Pacific island) always contained plenty of plump, brown, willing females. I couldn't make up my mind about this place.

Along the paths or in the fields, the naked children engaged in sex play the way animals do, touching and sniffing at one another, ignored by the adults. Quite a lot of the sex play was homosexual, and that made me think that perhaps there were no restrictions on sex. On the other hand, it was at the time of sexual maturity that people began to wear the tunic, a point in favor of modesty and sexual taboos. But what I saw made me doubt there were any.

I'd been walking beyond the fields into the orchards when I heard a sound. Ahead of me were a young boy and girl sprawled on the ground. Her tunic was pulled up and so was his. She was kneeling over him, straddling his chest. Then she slid down and sat on his erected organ, giving a little grunt as it pushed into her. A couple of rocking motions and it was all over, and both of them looked a little uncertain and unfinished. Then they laughed, got up and snatched some leaves from one of the trees to clean themselves, rubbing the leaves between their legs. They threw the leaves on the ground, clasped each other's hands and went back to the fields. There they parted, went back to work and seemed not to notice one another again.

What really shook me was that on their way back they spotted me, realized I'd been watching them, but gave no sign of embarrassment. In fact they both gave me what I can only describe as a smile of enticement, looking over their shoulders at me as they went back to work.

I'd been weeks without a woman, at first hurt and sick, later confused. In fact I'd been in such a state of confused frustration for the past few days that I was probably ready for some kind of emotional explosion. The explosion, after seeing those two kids rutting like animals, was a sexual one. But I wasn't interested in kids. I knew who I wanted, and if things were so free and easy here, I could at least enjoy her, and probably think a lot straighter afterward.

I walked across the field to where Augustine bent over a plant. I resisted a temptation to pat her uplifted buttock and instead greeted her, "Nagdeo."

She stood erect and smiled uncertainly at me, then frowned. She was as tall as I was and her sweat had made the grassy tunic cling to her breasts and thighs. I could hardly wait to get the dress off and see the black curve of her thigh. I'd had black women before, but they'd never lived up to my expectations of primitive passion. I found them cold and sad. But Augustine was different. I reached out my hand and took hers. I led her away from the field, into the orchard, picking a place not far from where the kids had been. Then I turned and put my arms around her.

She still had the uncertain smile on her face, but it left her and her blue eyes widened. "Don't be afraid," I said, but I could see she was not afraid. She was just very serious. She stood still and stolid, unresponding but unresisting. With my arms still around her, I pulled up her tunic until I could grab her bare buttocks in both hands. The butterfly rose from her shoulder and hovered over us. I waved my arm; it fluttered just out of reach.

"Donagdeo," she said. "Donagdeo." It was like another form of the greeting. Maybe it meant, "Let's go," or something, I told myself. But I knew I was wrong. Her expression as she said it was solemn. She stood absolutely still and whispered, "Donagdeo."

"Sure, to you too, baby," I said. I took her by the shoulders and tried to lower her to the ground. She was stiff. But she didn't fight. "Come on," I said. "We're not kids, let's not play coy." I decided that she was probably as strong as I was and if she didn't want it she could knock me down, and if she couldn't do that all she had to do was call out to the others, who weren't more than a hundred yards away. Probably she liked it a little rough, I thought, as I pushed her down to the ground and yanked up her tunic.

There were stretch marks on her belly. "You're not exactly a virgin," I mumbled. I pulled the tunic up beyond her breasts. It covered her face, and she lay still.

Her nipples were bright rust-colored against the black swelled breasts. She shuddered when I got one of them between my teeth. I thought what a great lay she would be if I could wait and do it right. But this time I couldn't wait. I knew I'd come the minute I got into her. But it wouldn't matter to her. She was used to primitive sex. Later I could impress her with technique. I grabbed her knees and pushed them upward and out as I kneeled up to her, keeping my mouth clamped onto her breast.

That was why I didn't notice them. I only felt something, the hair rising on my neck, a slight chill on my back. I raised my head and looked up to see a pair of legs planted in front of me. It was the bald man. To the side were more legs; all around us people stood. I threw my hands over my head, expecting a blow from them. But nobody moved. They just stood there watching.

"Look, she wants it, she's not resisting," I said, pointing to her. She lay quite still, her face still covered by her tunic, her body quivering slightly. None of them looked at her. They just looked at me, with the same grave expression she had worn. Nobody moved, nobody said anything. "Well, if she's your woman, one of you, come get her," I said. Nobody moved.

"Okay, you want to watch?" I said, and threw myself upon her. Nobody moved. Suddenly I felt sick. Something I had not felt for so long I hardly knew what it was—a wave of shame—passed through me. I felt it only as anger, sickening anger. I stood up. As soon as I did, the people fell back and started to walk back to the fields. I walked away, feeling like a fool with the tunic I wore still at a tilt with my waning erection. I went up the side of the hill beyond the trees, and watched a couple of them help Augustine up and lead her away.

She went straight across the field to a hol-ka (one of the little igloos). She crawled into it and stayed there the rest of the day. I didn't see her when I went to the la-ka to eat at sundown. And she left a gap among the spokes of our sleeping wheel that night. I didn't sleep much, and at dawn I saw her come in briefly, then leave again with the others. She was smiling and looked actually happy. Her smile was especially broad as she bowed toward me before going out to go to work.

I thought she was laughing at me. I suspected that they were all laughing at me. Savages, I told myself, laughing at me.

I don't excuse what I did then. It, like most of my life, was inexcusable. But I understand it. I was a throughly lost, dislocated man. For all I knew I was insane and living some kind of nightmare on an island in my demented head. Nothing made sense. I was in the midst of the inexplicable, minute by minute, all day long, with no hope of understanding where I was and waning hope of getting back to reality. It was like being suddenly struck blind and trying to find my way without help. Worse, because if I were blind I would know that beyond my blindness there existed a still familiar reality. But reality was, in fact, what no longer existed in any recognizable form. I was afraid, and fear turns very rapidly into cruelty. I wanted revenge.

I went out to the fields. I followed and I watched until she went off by herself, to one of the fallow fields. I waited while she dug a small hole, crouched over it, then filled the hole with dirt. Then I grabbed her, threw her down and rammed myself into her. I came, like a sneeze without pleasure or relief.

And I felt I had lost something again. Even lying in that dirt she had a kind of dignity I couldn't touch. I felt that I was the one who'd been humiliated. She looked steadily up at me, shook her head slowly and said, "Donagdeo." Her eyes flashed angrily, and she shook her head as if to clear it, got up quickly, brushing the dirt off her tunic and hurried away. Almost running, she pulled off her tunic as she hurried across the field to a hol-ka. She dropped the tunic on the ground and crawled inside.

I watched for a long time, but she didn't come out. When she ran away, I'd assumed she was going to tell the others and that they would gang up on me again. I'd been warned once. This time, I thought, they'd hurt me. I believed I'd probably bring the whole village down on me.

But nothing happened. A couple of hours later she was back in the fields working, moving in light dance-like steps as she stirred the ground with her hands and feet, loosening the dirt round a plant. No one seemed to notice me as I walked across the field, wandered through the orchards, then back toward the village again.

I stopped in front of a hol-ka. It was a small mound of clay and rocks, like an igloo, with a crawl tunnel leading into it. The entrance was covered by a mat. Just outside the entrance I saw a tunic, folded neatly on the ground. Evidently people entered a hol-ka naked. But what did they do there?

I walked a few yards to the next hol-ka. There was no tunic outside, no sign that the place was occupied. I looked around. No one was close by. I pulled off my tunic and crawled in. The short tunnel was narrow. I had to fall on my belly and move forward on my elbows. Then the tunnel went sharply downward. The place was actually a hole in the ground, covered with a rock and clay roof. It was completely dark inside and there was enough height to kneel but not to stand. By the earthy smell I recognized this as the place where I'd awakened after the accident, or, at least, one like this. I felt around the sides and top. Nothing. It was quite bare except for mats on the ground. I sat down on a mat. I sat still for about ten minutes, and then the place got to me. I was overcome with claustrophobic panic, and I frantically felt the walls until I found the opening. I crawled out too quickly and scraped my shoulders, emerging head first and blinking into the bright sunlight.

As I poked my head out, someone was passing by. It was the bald man, who hadn't spoken to me since he'd caught me with Augustine. He smiled at me, nodding approval, and said, "Nagdeo." I was sick of the sound of the word. I put on my tunic and straggled along the circular path, letting it take me inward toward the center of the village.

Along the path there were children and old people, tending plants and bushes which grew along the stone walls. Others sat weaving grass. Someone was always weaving grass into tunics, blankets, cups or mats. Some of them smiled and nodded as I passed; others remained absorbed in their work, silently, except for the occasional babble of a child which was usually answered with a gesture by an adult. I looked a little more closely at the walls as I slowly walked by. At first I thought they were covered with undifferentiated weeds, wild ivy and lichens. But now I saw there was too much variety for the growth to have occurred naturally. I knew very little about plants and flowers, having always considered any interest in them the province of lonely senile women, like the collecting of cats. But I was able to recognize some simple herbs, like sage and a species of thyme. I could see that the plants growing on and near the low stone walls were an incredible variety, almost no one like another, and that they were being carefully tended by people who were too young or too old to do much work in the fields.

As I was looking at a plant, Chil-sing came past me. I caught his arm and pointed to the herb. He spoke a word. Then I pointed to another herb, and he spoke the same word. I shook my head, pointing to one and the other as he repeated the word. Then suddenly he grinned, and nodded, and gave me two entirely different words.

We sat down in the middle of the path and began to talk. It would serve no purpose to describe this session of gestures, sounds, frustrations, charades. In fact it would be impossible to explain all the ways in which I finally conveyed my meaning to Chil-sing and how he answered me. This was the first of the really searching conversations—or call them lessons—we had. And how we communicated cannot be literally translated into English. Even after I became fluent in the Ata language, I found it impossible to translate directly into English, for many of the reasons which I have already outlined, and others besides. All talk which follows must be seen as a crude approximation of what we were able to communicate at the various stages of my understanding.

I can tell you how the breakthrough in this understanding came during this session with Chil-sing. I spoke in English with gestures and then, for no reason in particular, switched to words in other languages, whatever words I knew. And I discovered that some of the words in English were close enough to the Ata word to be understood. The same was true of words in Spanish, German, and the bit of Greek I knew. Over half the words Chil-sing used were completely inexplicable to me, and I somehow held the conviction that these words came from Asian or African languages that were utterly foreign to me. I asked him if this were true, and he shrugged and said he did not know.

The following dialogue is a condensation in English of what actually took nearly four hours to communicate, in the first real conversation I held.

"What is this island?"

"Ata."

"Where is it?"

"It is Ata."

"No, in what part of the world?"

"In the center of the world."

"But near what country? Near Mexico? Near Europe? Where?"

"I cannot say anything of countries. Ata is the center of the world."

"How did I get here?"

"Why you came is unknowable."

"Not why, how?"

"They are the same."

"Where did I come from? Who brought me here?"

He was silent at this question and looked at me for a while before he said, "Only you can answer that."

"What do you mean? I don't know who brought me here. I was in an accident. I woke up here."

He shook his head at me. "No one comes without seeking. You could not come here unless you wanted to."

"Where did you find me?"

"On the shore."

"On the shore of the ocean? Where?"

He pointed toward the east, toward the beach where the sunrise bath took place every six to nine days.

"Who found me?"

"I did. And Salvatore." That was the bald man's name.

"How did you happen to find me?"

"We were looking for you."

"You expected me?"

"Yes."

"How did you know I was coming?"

"Augustine knew."

"How did she know? Who told her?"

"Nagdeo."

"I thought nagdeo was a greeting, like good morning."

"It is."

"But you say it is a person?"

"I don't know."

"Who is he? Where can I find him and talk to him?"

At this Chil-sing just laughed, and despite our continued talking I could not make any sense of his earnest attempts to explain the word to me.

"How did you come here?"

"I was born here."

"But the others, did they come from other places, as I did?"

Chil-sing shook his head, then looked uncertain. Some had, but not very many. "It is very hard to come here, as you know."

"They must have," I told him. "That explains why your language contains words borrowed from other languages."

At that Chil-sing laughed. "Oh, no," he said. "Oh, no."

"Explain yourself. What do you mean?"

"I don't know. I cannot explain." His young face looked puzzled. "I am not very wise yet. If you listen in the la-ka at night you will soon learn all the answers to your questions."

"Is your treasure kept in the la-ka?"

"Treasure?"

"The riches of your people. The precious ornaments used in the dances."

"Oh, yes." He frowned as if uncertain. "Our treasure is kept in the la-ka." He pushed back his golden curls and looked apologetic. "But please . . . I would please like to stop talking now."

"Why? What are you hiding? Why are you such a silent people? Is there a taboo against talking?" It took a long time to explain the word taboo to him, and even then he did not understand the word, could not seem to imagine what it meant.

"No, there is no taboo. Nothing is taboo." He looked

quite shocked and puzzled, unable to assimilate the concept of something forbidden.

"Then why do you all remain so silent?"

"Talking too much is donagdeo." He grinned and backed off from me. I saw him hop the stone walls and hurry toward the hol-kas, pulling off his tunic as he ran. I sat down on the path and leaned against the wall, closing my eyes and thinking. I must have dozed off. When I woke up a half hour or so later he was walking past me, arm in arm with Augustine. It was sunset.

When they saw me, they stopped to wait for me. I got up, my eyes meeting Augustine's. Hers looked neutral and serene. I moved as though to walk behind them, but they made a space between them and we walked three abreast, in silence, as usual.

Then Augustine began to hum softly and Chil-sing joined her. Others walking behind us joined in, rather absentmindedly, immediately breaking into rich harmonies, which died off into whispers. We stopped at the pool and scooped water up to our faces, rubbed our hands together and sprinkled what was left on the tree roots as we ducked under the branches of the great tree.

A few people were already in the center of the cone near the fire, feeding one another from the pots. Others were carrying in bits of fruit. A child came up to me and stuck a sprig of sage in my hair. It was all very friendly and loving and gay, and completely frustrating to me. There was not very much food and it took a long time to pass it around in this playful way. I would have been glad for a stiff drink and a cigarette. I'd read somewhere that every culture in the world has always discovered some method of intoxication, be it hemp or alcohol. I wondered if these bastardized rejects of various cultures—for that is how I now saw them—had not even reached a sufficient level of culture to be able to get drunk.

I sulked, I suppose, letting people bring me bites of food but offering none in return. "Hurry up," I told them. "Let's get on with it." They understood me, but went on as they were doing until everyone stopped eating and was seated.

People tended to sit according to their ages. The infants were held by boys and girls, down in the center of the cone near the fire. Behind them sat slightly older children, Chil-sing among them, and behind them the adults. Augustine sat in the back near the top of the cone, her head resting against one of the beams that pointed to the sky. The very oldest people were carried down to sit near the fire with the infants.

Salvatore sat with his eyes half closed near the fire. The black bird flew to the top of the tent poles, then glided downward in sweeps above the heads of the people as they quieted down. When they were quiet, it landed on Salvatore's shoulder, and Salvatore began to speak.

What I reproduce here is my limping translation of what he said. It lacks the purity and directness of the Ata language, and also its complexity, which was revealed only in these sessions, never in the language of everyday acts. But I had finally broken through, and, although the story I give here was a version arrived at after much work, I understood the sense of the story, got most of the words, at that first hearing.

"Nagdeo without beginning. Nagdeo without end. Nagdeo forever, our home."

At the end of each phrase the people repeated a word

or two, but I will leave out these responses.

"But the day came when a piece of the sun fell to the ocean. It fell and floated on the ocean. It separated itself into earth and water and plants and animals. It was no longer sun, but each of its parts was a part of the sun and a sign of the sun. And all parts, earth and water and plants and animals, were content in their division, content in their expression of the sun, content to be a single part multiplying itself under the light of the sun, striving and being, as a sign of the sun but never true sun, lost to the form of the true sun."

I could see the lips of the people moving in silent imitation. They all knew the story by heart.

"Until the single multiple signs formed the human part. And the human part of the sun was not content. The human part suffered because within it was the knowledge of the fall from the sun and the yearning to return.

"It knew and it did not know. It suffered and yearned. It suffered and yearned for what it did not know. And out of its suffering and yearning grew the cry of the people, yearning to know the way back to the sun.

"And the sun took pity on the people, and when they fell asleep, the sun shone through the sleep and lit up the world of sleep and showed them the way. In silent light of sleep the people saw that as there was a law of gravity there was also a law of light and that the law of light was stronger than the law of gravity.

"And the people obeyed the light of sleep, and they kept the light within them, and stood in the light of sleep both waking and sleeping until the light surrounded them and filled them. And they became the light. And as the sun shone on them, they shone back, and were lifted as light and shot as rays of light. And gravity was overcome and the people of light returned to the sun where they shine and flame eternally.''

I had been listening with my eyes closed, concentrating on the words. I opened my eyes. Salvatore stood in front of the fire. The spokes of a gold crown radiated from his head with almost blinding glow. Then a quick motion, and the crown was gone.

"Eternally,'' repeated the people. Then they all rose, said, "Nagdeo, nagdeo, nagdeo,'' and began to leave the tent.

The next day I approached Salvatore. He absolutely refused to discuss the gold crown. His face remained blank when I spoke of it.

"Did you understand what you heard last night?'' he asked.

"Yes,'' I said, contemptuously. "I understand that you worship the sun, a common thing among primitive people.'' He looked at me but said nothing. "And you believe dreams are real happenings. Isn't that right?'' He nodded.

"Do you know,'' I said, as he picked up a half-finished mat and started weaving, "that the sun is only a star, like all the other stars you see in the sky at night? There are millions of suns and millions of planets all spinning around the suns and . . . '' I wished that my knowledge of astronomy were greater. The old man listened to me and said nothing. "You really believe that man's distinguishing characteristic is his desire to return to the sun? The sun is a ball of fire. If this planet moved a bit closer to it, we'd all be burned up!'' He nodded. "Then why do you cling to these senseless myths?'' He didn't answer.

I decided there was really no point in attacking him on these grounds but rather on the question of dreams. "Yours is a life based on delusion and hallucination," I began, but he looked so sad and depressed at these words that I gave up for the rest of that day.

In the morning, when everyone in our ka got up and began the recital of what they had dreamed the night before, "in the world of sleep lit by the sun," I interrupted them with a little recital of my own. "Dreams," I said, "are not real, like this is real." I touched my arm and then hit one of the branches of the ka. "They are hallucinations, mental enactments of desires. Dreams are the guardian of sleep. You dreamed of a plum because you were hungry. You dreamed I was pulling your leg off because the bruise on your leg aches where you bumped into the wall yesterday."

"Yes, that is perhaps true," said Chil-sing.

"But you believe in these dreams. You think they are reality?"

"Yes, they are reality."

"But they happen only in your head!"

There is little point in repeating the endless arguments with which I started every morning. There was no question about it, no doubt at all that for these people, reality consisted of dreams and their waking life was an illusion. They had reversed everything. At one point, in exasperation, I slapped Chil-sing hard across the face and said, "Look, isn't that real, my real hand hit your real face, and it really hurt."

"Yes, it hurt," said Chil-sing. "But that does not matter. What matters is that it is donagdeo for you to be angry and hit me."

The translation of the word was quite clear now, although there is, of course, no such word in English, or any other language. The word nagdeo, which was a greeting, a prayer, a benediction, whatever, roughly meant something like "good dreams," but not really that. It was something more like valuable dreams or enlightening dreams. To call something donagdeo was to say that it was not productive of good, valuable, or enlightening dreams, dreams which showed the way back—to the sun.

All kinds of things were donagdeo. Anger was donagdeo, and so was eating too much or not eating enough, or talking too much. The list grew and grew.

But beyond that, every act had become ritualized to serve the dramas of their dream life, which in turn dictated their waking life. The very plan of the village had occurred in a dream of someone long ago, no one could remember when. I pointed out to Chil-sing that everyone walked at least an extra mile getting to the la-ka because of the circular paths, but he said that is how the dream said it should be done, and it would remain that way unless superseded by another very strong dream.

"If your dream told you to kill me, would you do it?" I demanded.

"It would not tell me that."

"Why? How do you know?"

"To kill is donagdeo. It would not tell me to do what is donagdeo."

"My dreams do. In my dreams I must kill dark things that . . . " I stopped. I had no intention of joining the morning ritual of telling my dreams. Chil-sing looked at me uncertainly.

"You told me," I said, "that there were no taboos here. Your whole life is run by the most primitive taboos, the most reactionary and restrictive."

"No," said Chil-sing. "Nothing is taboo."

"But everything is donagdeo. Same thing."

"No, it is not the same. Nothing is forbidden. But who would want to do what is donagdeo? Who would want to ruin his chance to find the way?"

"How do you know what is donagdeo? The old ones like Salvatore tell you, don't they? They make rules, taboos."

Chil-sing looked puzzled again. "Salvatore is a strong dreamer, a good guide."

"You see. Taboo."

Chil-sing shook his head. "But each person finds for himself what is donagdeo. To force anyone to do or not to do something is also donagdeo. Nothing is forbidden. Nothing is taboo. But I listen to Salvatore because he is usually right."

I nearly exploded with exasperation. "If I could only get you to believe that beyond this island there is a fantastic world, full of wonders you never could dream of. Places where people don't have to exist on leaves and berries and work all day, where . . . "

At this point Chil-sing usually withdrew. But each time I told him, he sounded a bit more curious. Once when I was haranguing him, we heard the roar of an airplane. He froze, and so did everyone else around us.

"Why did you do that?" I asked.

"So the people in the noisy bird won't see us."

"How do you know there are people in it?"

"Someone saw them in a dream."

"And why don't you want them to see you?"

"Someone knew it in a dream."

"I want to attract the attention of a plane so that it will come and get me and take me off this island and back to civilization. Would you stop me?"

Chil-sing bit his lip. "We would watch you, as we watched you when you tried to force Augustine."

"And if I didn't stop?"

"To force you would be donagdeo. But I think they fly too high to see you anyway."

"Then why do you freeze to avoid being seen?"

"Habit," he said.

"Let me tell you something," I said. "If we could attract the attention of that plane, we could get food and clothes and thousands of things you never dreamed of. And you wouldn't have to work in the fields all day, to have them. And at night, you wouldn't sit on the hard steps of the la-ka and watch the repetition of some old story—you could enjoy plays and pictures that would make your dreams seem pale. You could trade the treasure of the la-ka for many things. Why don't Salvatore and the other old ones tell you this? Why should I lie to you about it? You know I'm telling the truth. They don't want you to learn about the outside world because they'd lose control of this one."

Day after day I kept at him. I figured that the only ones I could get to were the young ones. The older ones were completely set and unapproachable. And I would need help if I were ever to manage to get away from here.

I thought Augustine must be a key figure in all of this.

But it was a long time before I felt I could approach her. Finally one day I did. She had come back early from the fields and was walking along the path, her eyes fixed in a faraway look that told me she was thinking over her latest dream. I stepped out in front of her.

She stopped and faced me without any expression.

"I want to talk to you," I said. She nodded, and we sat down on the stone wall under a fig tree.

"I'm sorry for what I did," I began.

She nodded. "You should go to the hol-ka," she said, "just to be sure."

"Sure of what?"

"It would help you."

"How? I don't understand. It feels to me like a tomb."

"The hol-ka is to help us when we have gone very far from nagdeo, or when we are afraid we might. There we go naked back into our mother."

"And you come out reborn."

"And begin again," she smiled. "I go often . . . "

"Yes, every day, I notice."

" . . . because I so often stumble. I am so far from . . . "

"Nonsense," I told her. "You've got some kind of puritannical obsession with . . . " Then I wasted an hour trying to explain what I meant by puritannical. She just kept smiling and shaking her head. "It's that you feel guilty because I raped you and . . . " Another hour on guilt. I was practically yelling when I finally said, "You people are imprisoned by your superstitions!"

And she only shrugged and said, "Perhaps."

"I can't get any of you to argue with me."

"Arguing is . . . "

"Don't tell me . . . donagdeo."

She laughed and nodded.

I was tired and irritable like a sulking child. "I really wanted to ask you about the dream that told you I would come here. Please tell me that dream, every detail of it."

It was sunset, and we got up to walk to the la-ka. She put her arm through mine and told me as we walked, keeping her eyes straight ahead as if she read her words in the air before us.

"I was walking on the beach. I walked back and forth on the sand looking out to the sea watching for the sunrise. Behind me stood all the people of Ata, and behind them stood many, many more people who were not of Ata. All looked out to sea. They were waiting for something. We all waited. The sea turned red, a dark earth red. And from the sea came a great cry, a howl from a creature not human. I could see the creature in the red waves. It was a terrible, monstrous beast. I was afraid. But I knew what I must do. I waded out into the rust-colored sea. I waded further and further out to where the monster thrashed and howled. And when I came close, the monster reached out and grasped me. It tried to pull me into the deep red sea. But I kept my eyes on the sun rising out of the red sea behind the monster. And tightly as it gripped me I began to inch backward toward the shore. The monster howled and tightened its grip, but I kept my eyes on the rising sun and I kept stepping back to the shore, inch by inch.

"Finally I reached dry sand, just as the sun emerged from the water. I fell on the sand, and the thing gripping me fell upon me. In the light of the risen sun, I looked and saw that it was no longer a monster but a man. He rose up and the people of Ata, still standing on the beach, said

'Welcome. We have been waiting for you.' And from the head of the man came a bright light, like the rays of the sun. The man turned his head to look at us, and turned the bright light upon us, lighting up the people of Ata so that they could be seen by the many people who stood behind."

I waited for her to go on, but she was through. "You dreamed of a man who tried to pull you into a rust-red sea. How long before I came since you lay with a man?"

She looked at me. "A long time."

I thought her pathetic, a striking woman, but no longer young. It had been a long time since anyone had taken her into the orchard. "You dreamed this dream because you wanted to lie with a man."

"Perhaps," she said, refusing to argue.

We walked on quietly for a while. Then she said, "After I had dreamed the dream three times. I told it in the la-ka as is our custom."

"And so it became official dogma."

"Dogma?"

"Never mind. You told your dream and then you found me. There is no connection."

"In the dream," she said, "I saw the face of the man in the sunlight. It was your face."

"Are you sure you didn't dream this after you found me?"

"Sure," she said. "I waited for you."

"So you believe your dream brought me here?"

"No. Oh, no," she said. "No one can bring you here. You must want it with your whole soul. You wanted it."

"I did not."

"You cried from the depths of yourself to come here."

She looked at me admiringly. "Still it is not easy. You must be a very strong dreamer."

We had arrived at the pool. She bent low, scooped up water to sprinkle on herself and on the tree, then disappeared under the branches.

We ate in the usual way and then sat down. That night the storyteller was a younger one, a boy who had just begun to wear a tunic. He sat down beside the fire, waited for everyone to be quiet, then cleared his throat and began.

"A boy lived for many years in a ka. Every day he wanted to look upon the sun, but he could not, for to look directly at the sun would make him blind. Instead, when the sun went down, the boy looked at the moon, which had taken a bit of the sun's light, enough to show to the boy what he must do.

"When the boy rose in the morning, he said to his kin. 'The moon brings a message from the sun, which is that I must find my mother and my father. Are you my mother? Are you my father?'

"The people of his ka answered that they were not. So the boy left his ka. All day long he walked through the village, through the orchards, over the hill, beside the river, and down to the ocean, asking every woman he saw, 'Are you my mother?' and every man, 'Are you my father?'

"Finally a woman and a man answered, 'Out of our bodies came yours.' And the boy said, 'Then you are my mother and father,' but the man and woman shook their heads.

"And the boy said, 'How will I find my mother and my father,' and the man and the woman said, 'You must travel a long way by the light of both the sun and the moon, and sometimes there will be neither sun nor moon, but only darkness. Yet you must not fear the darkness because it too can tell you things. Never rest in your search until . . . "

At this point I got up from my seat. I was about midway up in the cone. By the time I had walked down to the fire, the boy's voice was stilled and all the people were looking at me.

"Augustine had a dream about me," I started. "She dreamed I came out of the sea, and that all of you were waiting for me." I paused and waited but there was no reaction aside from a few nods. "She dreamed that from my head a great light came, shining on all of you." Again I waited, and the people leaned forward. "Now I shall tell you what that light was. It was the light of reason, the great light of mankind. It meant that I was sent here to make a light in the darkness in which you have lived for so long, a light that would drive out superstition and teach you reality, a light to take you out of your dreams."

At that, there was a sharp murmur from some of the people, but many of the children watched me, fascinated.

"I come from a place where men fly in the air, not only in their dreams but in real life. You have seen them. A place where the food is so sweet and rich and varied that none of your dreams could contain it, and where most people do not need to labor in the fields to get it. It is a place full of waking wonders, real wonders that remain, that are solid and permanent, not the fantasies and hallucinations of dreams. And I want to go back there! Who wants to go with me?"

"I do, I do," piped a couple of the smallest children,

but from the older people came a kind of mass groan.

"You are told in this boy's dream to seek your true mother and father. How do you know that your true mother and father are not out there in my world? How do you know that the old people of Ata are not trying to keep you from finding your true mother and father? Out there, away from this island, in the great world are a thousand times Ata, the whole population of Ata many times over. And there things are real and people do not live on fantasies."

People were getting up and leaving. I imagined them running to the hol-kas. "Look at them," I said, "running to hide in a hole in the ground because I try to tell them about the larger world." One of the children laughed.

I saw Augustine standing up near the top of the cone. She was as still as a statue. I could not see her face, black against the black sky. I did not want to see even her figure standing over me. When I looked at her, all my self-righteous determination ebbed out of me and left me empty.

For, of course, I was lying. It was easy to talk about bringing the blessings of so-called civilization to Ata. Ata would probably gain a jet-strip, a gambling casino and a set of slums from which these people could go out each day to serve the tourists. It could even become another navy base. If the people were not so ignorant, I thought, nor so reluctant to argue, they could easily have made my little speech sound ridiculous.

My real plan was to get possession of the precious stones and metals they used in their rituals and return to the world with a new name, a new identity and plenty to live on for the rest of my life. But I couldn't do it alone. I needed help, and I would have to promise something to get that help.

I kept talking. "You are being held prisoners of superstition. Follow me and I will save you."

Soon all had left but about fifteen children. Chil-sing was the oldest. I sent five away who were too little to be of any use.

"How far are we from the nearest land?" I asked.

"There are some other islands to the west," answered the boy who had told the story.

"No, I mean a continent, a large piece of land." All the children looked blank. "Have you never seen ships? What about airplanes? You know what they are. Did none of them ever land here?" The children shook their heads. "I want to leave here," I told them. "I want to go back to the great land. If you help me, I will take you with me."

They spoke all at once, assuring me that they wanted to go and would help me.

"It will mean going against the older ones," I warned them. "You will have to disobey them."

"We can do what we want," said Chil-sing. "There are no taboos here."

"Tomorrow we will begin," I said. I thought it best to say nothing about the treasure yet.

The children cheered. I looked up. Augustine was still standing high above us. Then she turned and disappeared over the rim of the cone.

The children and I slept in the la-ka. The next morning we began a thorough exploration of the island. It took us about five days, and revealed nothing of any interest. The only beach was the one used for bathing. Around the rest of the island were cliffs. We spent some time on the beach wading out nearly half a mile at low tide, calculating how to build a boat to take us away from the island.

It seems laughable, but it was a sign of my nearly total derangement that I seriously considered such a thing, I, a perfect example of a modern man, who knew no more than where to press the starter of my car; I was going to build a boat and put out to sea. (Of course, I had no intention of taking the children with me.) There were virtually no tools of any kind except for digging sticks and bones. After a few days of lashing together fallen logs with braided grass, I gave up the idea and watched while the children played in the surf on the raft we produced.

The only answer was to attract the attention of a passing airplane. The children and I started signal fires on top of the hill and on other rises all over the island. But the fires always went out quickly, whether through lack of attention or through being put out by the older people, I wasn't sure. Occasionally I carefully brought up the question of the treasure. The children seemed confused about what I meant, but were not averse to taking anything I wanted along with us.

No one seemed to be paying any attention to us. Everything went on as usual. Grain and legumes were being harvested and root vegetables planted. Food was prepared for storage on the steps of the la-ka; a few steps were already full.

The days were shorter, and the air crisper. Every evening the usual procession to the la-ka took place. The usual eating, singing and dream-telling took place. The children and I always waited until everyone had left. Then we came in and finished the food (they always left some for us) while I told stories of electric lights, subways, ice cream and television. We continued to sleep in the la-ka because I was afraid that, for all their seeming gentleness, the people might try to hurt me if it were necessary to prevent my leaving. Here, with my ten hostages around me, I felt safe.

The children slept fitfully, often starting and moaning. I slept little, if at all. The old nightmares had come back with redoubled terror and when they were not there I was killing Connie, endlessly, in slow motion. I suspected someone of poisoning the food left for us and began eating fruit I picked myself. But the nightmares continued, bursting on me every time I closed my eyes. I began to feel that the island was a trap where I would go mad and die.

Instead of sleeping, I spent the nights searching the la-ka, where I was sure the treasure was hidden between rituals. I dug dozens of holes, rifled through pots of grain and lifted every stone that surrounded the fire pit. But I found nothing.

Whenever a plane flew over we fanned our fires and signaled, but all the planes flew too high and too fast; we couldn't even see them, and they came seldom. We were not on any regularly traveled routes.

Then an extraordinary thing happened. The little girl I had standing lookout on the hill screamed and waved according to our pre-arranged signal. I could hardly believe the signal; it meant a ship was coming. She lit a fire while the rest of us ran to the beach.

It looked like a big ship, black and dingy looking. I was sure that after our fire was lit it changed course and headed for the island. I stood on the beach watching it while the children pulled off their tunics and waved them as signals while the smoke rose from the hill.

The ship came nearer and nearer. Then suddenly, it seemed to stop and rock uncertainly, as if suspended. And then just as suddenly, decisively, it turned back on course and steamed away. I was stunned. "They saw us, I know they did!" I said, and the children agreed. Chil-sing stood looking thoughtful. We walked back toward the village.

Before we neared the fields we could see that something had happened. People were lying all about, as if shot down in the midst of their work, in the fields, on the paths. Chil-sing walked beside me nodding his head slowly.

"Are they dead?" I asked. But even as I said it I saw one pick herself up and crawl toward a hol-ka. "What's happened?"

"I saw this once before," said Chil-sing. "When I was very young. That time it was a helicopter."

"What do you know about helicopters?" I asked, but he paid no attention.

"A helicopter." he went on, "came out from a ship. It was looking for someone lost at sea. It saw Ata. It came down close. It was going to land here." He paused. "And so Ata disappeared—sank into the sea. Disappeared—like in a dream."

"How?"

"The people, together, made it so. In the eyes of the person in the helicopter or the people on the ship, Ata melted into the sea like . . . " He shrugged.

" . . . a mirage," I said. "How is it done?"

He shrugged again. "It is very hard. But we have always done it. You may even have heard of it." He looked at me expectantly until I admitted there were long standing legends about an island that had sunk into the sea. "You see. But it is very hard. The people are exhausted now. They will not be able to do it again for a while. If another ship comes, we will get it."

"But how often does a ship come?"

"This was the first I have seen."

I sat down feeling as exhausted and as lifeless as the people lying in the fields. "How do you know about helicopters?"

Chil-sing shrugged. "From our dreams, of course. It is from our dreams that we know the stories you tell us of the great world are true. We have seen it— in our dreams." He waited for a minute and then he said, "And we have seen others that you did not tell us. Things that are wonders of horror."

"Then why do you stick with me?"

"I don't know," said Chil-sing. "Maybe you are the reality, and dreams are only dreams. From the beginning of time the kin of Ata have kept the way. Maybe your way is better. Otherwise, why did you come to Ata?"

That night as we lay down in the la-ka, my eyes began to close and my nightmare figures—always waiting in the shadows—began oozing upward toward me. I jumped, woke and found myself surrounded. I threw up my arms, but nothing happened.

Salvatore, Aya, Augustine, Sbgai looked down at me. Around them were six or seven of the oldest inhabitants of the island, two of whom could barely stand. Behind them my gang of sleepy-eyed children were getting up.

Chil-sing stepped up beside me and said, "He is my friend. If you hurt him, I will fight you."

Salvatore shook his head. "Where do you learn words like that? Why should we bring evil dreams upon ourselves?" He turned to me. "We came to talk to you. May all sit down?"

Everyone sat near the glowing red coals of the fire. The oldest, it seemed, was to be the spokesman. It was the sexless, dried up creature from our ka, whom they called Tam. He usually leaned on a small donkey, but had left the animal outside. In a quavering voice he said, "If our island is discovered, our way of life will perish."

"That's true," I said. "And a better way of life will take its place." I smiled at the children and nodded confidently, but when I turned back to look at the old creature, his level glance made me squirm.

"No," he said. "No." Then quite suddenly, he switched to a halting French. "I was chosen to speak to you because I came here as you did, from the outside. It happens rarely. Augustine's mother, a great singer who died when Augustine was born, did so. Chil-sing's grandfather, a Korean monk, was another. But it happens rarely. You and I are the only ones now. I came in 1914, out of a trench, bathed in the blood of young men who were blown apart faster than these hands could patch them up. Here my medical skills have proven largely useless, since Atans do not bring upon themselves the dis-eases of the outside world. Only once did my skill do anything here: I managed to save Augustine's life when her mother died. I believe that I came here in order to do that."

"It is a very hard thing," said Salvatore, "a very great thing, to come from the outside. That is why we were so grateful that you came, because we saw you as part of the fulfillment of our purpose."

The Frenchman switched back to Ata Language. "We

thought you came as I did, willingly, with your whole heart. But that does not seem to be true."

"It is not true," I agreed. "Your black witch seems to have got me here."

Augustine said nothing. I got up and climbed to the fourth level of steps. The old Frenchman followed.

"Ata is the only hope. It alone stands apart from the way of life you and I left. You and I know better than anyone how precarious . . . if you destroy Ata, you destroy . . ."

"I don't want to destroy it. I don't give a damn what you do here, but I want out."

"We will try to get you out," said Salvatore. "That is what we came to tell you."

"How?"

"There is a way. But you will have to be patient. We cannot do it yet."

"When?" I demanded.

"In the spring. It can only be done in the spring."

"Why? Why should I believe you?"

He shrugged. "We will do it as we have done in the past when exiles have been sent from Ata. But it is very hard."

"Harder than making Ata invisible?"

He didn't blink an eye. "Much harder. It can be done, I think. But not until spring, after the winter fast."

"By that time I'll . . ."

"We promise to do it. Only be patient. We know we must do it to keep our way of life. You must see that we want this as much as you want to get out."

"No deal," I said.

"What more can we do?"

"Give me the treasure." There was a moment of silence. "The jewels, the gold. I can put it to better use. I need it. I can't go back without it." The silence deepened. "Look, those are my terms. It can't matter to you. You probably stole them off shipwrecks anyway. They don't really belong to you."

Salvatore frowned. "You can have anything you want."

"Okay. Turn them over. Now. To show good faith. Then I'll wait till spring and I won't cause any more trouble."

Salvatore shrugged and turned up his hands, palms outward. "I do not understand what you want."

I thought I caught a look on the face of the old Frenchman. "Okay, you tell him what I mean. You know what I'm talking about. The crown. The rubies. The pearl. The diamonds Aya poured over her head. Whatever else. The fetishes used in the ceremonies. They don't know that these things will bring the money I need to live when I leave here. Make it clear to them that I must have these things."

The old crone spoke like a squeaky hinge. I could understand most of what he said. He didn't seem to be trying to trick me, but was honestly trying to explain to them what I meant. At the end of each sentence, they all turned and looked at me. Even the children's mouths hung open.

"Tell me," said the squeaky-voiced old creature. "Tell me, you saw these things during the telling of the stories in the la-ka?"

"Yes, right here, I saw. I'm not blind."

"You saw what?" asked Aya, stroking her white cat,

83

which kept making hissing noises at me. "Please, tell us."

"I saw the kid with the pearl in his mouth. I saw them passing rubies. I saw you," I motioned to Salvatore, "with your crown on your head. I haven't found where you hide it between performances. But wherever it is, you probably have more. Don't try to lie. Augustine admitted it. She told me that you kept your treasure in the la-ka."

Then Tam, the old Frenchman, made a terrible mistake. He smiled. It was almost a laugh, a slight breathy sound behind the smile.

I only meant to scare him. I was furious, but I felt quite in control of myself because I thought I had won. I simply reached out to give him a backhanded slap across the face, to frighten him, to show them all that I meant business.

It was the last time I ever struck a blow of any kind at anyone.

He was so old and frail that he must have weighed less than any of the children. He was one of the ones who was usually carried down to sit near the fire in the la-ka. At a bare touch of my hand he lost his balance. He fell head down in a heap, across three steps. His head struck the lowest step. The smile was still on his face. We didn't have to touch him to see he was dead.

We all stood looking down at him. Then Chil-sing gave a kind of growl which rose to a yell, and sprang at me. I think he would have killed me. But Salvatore stepped between us, and both he and Child-sing went down in front of me. I ran up the steps. Augustine was right behind me, followed by the rest of the children, who made noises like wolves about to tear me apart. When we reached the top of the cone I tripped and fell in front of the entrance. I expected that Augustine would be on me, but that was not what happened. She turned to face the boys and girls, spreading out her arms and legs to try to receive any blow meant for me, at the same time saying, "Donag-deo," over and over. I jumped up and ran.

It was completely dark. I had never seen the sky so black. I ran like a blind man, with my hands outstretched in front of me. Every few steps I tripped and fell, over tree roots, stone walls, over my own feet. I ran across the fields toward the hill from which I had first seen the ocean. Every few steps upward I fell. I climbed like an ape, on all fours, feeling my way with my hands. There was a wild, roaring sound in my head. I thought it was the growls of people following me. I imagined that Chil-sing and the other young ones had gotten past Augustine, had aroused the village, and that all were coming after me to tear me apart.

I judged them all by myself, assuming that their patience and gentleness covered pent-up rage which would now be unleashed upon the murderer. The twice murderer.

I had never felt any guilt about Connie's death. But now, I had killed twice. Two accidents? Now they would follow me and kill me: quick, primitive justice. I thought I could hear them calling back and forth to one another as they searched the fields and orchards for me. I was terrified, yet in a way I hoped they would hurry up and find me, and get it over with.

At the top of the hill, I fell forward on the grass, my eyes closed, my arms hugging my knees, waiting, expecting at any moment to hear them coming. I wouldn't run anymore. I was too tired. I only wanted to sleep. But I was afraid I would dream. I lay shivering until the roar in my ears became the night wind, and the voices, the calls of birds. I sat up and looked around. The sky was a lighter black, and I could see the village as a series of black forms. Gradually the sky lightened. But the village remained still, not a sign of any person.

As the sky took on its first tinge of blue, the people began coming out of the tents. But they did not turn outward toward the fields. They began to walk the spiral paths inward toward the la-ka. Soon all the paths were empty again, and the bright dawning sun lit what looked like an empty village, appearing and disappearing in tricks before my aching eyes. The sky brightened in utter silence, except for the birds. I imagined the people were meeting to decide what to do about me.

Then I heard a thin stream of sound, a thread of unison melody, carried to me in fragments by the wind. And as I kept my eyes on the area of the la-ka, I saw the people begin to come out, in ones and twos, following the spiral paths, slowly winding outward. I saw only snatches of them through the bushes and trees lining the walls, a steady procession.

As they neared the outer spiral of the village, I could see those in the lead more clearly. I saw Chil-sing's golden hair flash in the sunlight. He and the other young ones walked two by two, carrying something between them. I knew it was the body of the old man, the only person on the island who had come to it as I had. How much I could have learned from him, and now it was too late.

I watched them cross the fields, going away from the

hill where I was, going toward the ocean to the east, where the sun was rising. Of course, they were going to bury their dead before they dealt with me, but I'd been too self-centered to realize that they would think of that before they would think of what to do with me. They would have plenty of time for me after they had given old Tam a proper funeral.

I lay on top of the hill, dozing in the sun, as a cat dozes, half alert, never descending into that deep sleep where my shadows waited for me.

After a couple of hours, I saw them coming back. This time the leaders were the old ones and the infants, carried or helped by the young. They wound their way inward to the la-ka and stayed there the whole day except for the brisk traffic between the la-ka and the hol-kas, which were constantly occupied, one person crawling in as soon as another came out.

When it was dark, I climbed down the hill and gathered fruit, which I took back up the hill to eat. It was cold. I crouched in the shelter of rocks, dozing, always with one ear cocked for the sound of a search party. At dawn, I peered over the edge of the hill, waiting to see what they would do. The people came out to the fields in their usual way, working and dancing, as if nothing had happened. Only one thing was unusual. It seemed to me that every time Augustine straightened up from her work, she shaded her eyes and looked upward toward the hill. I made sure that she would not see me.

I spent three days this way. By the third day I was feverish and coughing, trembling constantly. Of course, they were not going to come looking for me. They did not need to. They knew that sooner or later I would have to come down. I had begun to hallucinate. The grass began to look like sharp knives. The stones were gross, half-decayed faces. I huddled between two rocks, and the twigs which grew around them writhed like snakes. I looked at them without moving, knowing they were not real.

And I saw Tam, the dead Frenchman, standing before me with the smile on his face, the smile with which he had died. He shook his head, gave a very typical French shrug, as if to deprecate a situation which was taken too seriously. "J'étais très vieux." Then he switched back to Ata language and said, "We never mourn for those who go Home, my kin."

My head jerked upward. I must have dozed. The sun had already set behind the hill and my teeth were chattering. My eyes burned and my body felt as though it were being lifted by hundreds of tiny explosions going on inside of it. I was very sick. I would die that night, I felt sure.

My body twitched and shook, but my brain was very clear. I was going to die, again, as I had been going to die when my car plunged off the road. This time I was moved toward no animal howl of fear. I was afraid, yes, but I also thought it right that I should die. And since it was right that I should die, my death should be accomplished in the proper manner. I thought of walking toward the sunset, to the cliffs above the ocean, and jumping over, but I quickly rejected that. I probably couldn't make it to the other side of the island. Besides, there was only one proper way to die, and there was no use delaying any longer. If I delayed too long, I would die wrong, here, alone, seeing delusions. I would die as I had always lived, in delusion.

My proper death was waiting for me.

I got up and began to stagger down the hill. My memory of that walk is dim. I believe that at times I was not really conscious, that I simply pushed on like a sleep-walker. Sometimes I found myself on the ground, although I did not remember falling. I picked myself up and went on. I bumped against stone walls as I went round and round, spiraling inward until I came to the pool. I went down on my knees before the pool and submerged my head in it. When I got up again, the water ran off my head, down over my body. I remembered to shake a few drops onto the roots of the tree as I ducked past. Then I was at the entrance to the la-ka.

They were all there, in complete silence, waiting, as I had known they would be. Not a head turned as I started down the steps. All watched the fire, which blazed high. Before the fire stood Augustine, her black arms folded in front of her. Something gleamed in her hand. I thought it was a knife, the first metal I had seen on the island except for Salvatore's crown. The knife, I thought, was for me.

As I walked down the steps, my mind went completely blank. I had no idea what I would do.

When I reached Augustine, I tripped, and fell on my knees. I stayed there, with my head sunk on my chest. Somewhat numbly, I expected the knife to plunge into my neck. I began to mumble, but my voice carried and echoed in the silence. "I killed the old one. Before that I killed a woman. But these murders are the least of my crimes. I have never done anything good. I am an empty man. Not a real person. I gave away what was real in me long ago. I sold it. For nothing. I am nothing. I am not fit to live." The words came from my mouth, without my intending to say them, without my thinking them. But as each word was spoken, I knew it was true.

I waited for the knife. Something cool touched the back of my neck. I waited. Nothing happened. I raised my head and looked into Augustine's face. It was lit with the radiance of the fire and with something else. Her blue eyes shone with tears. Her arms were still folded in front of her. There was nothing in her hand, nothing but the gleam of her black skin in the light from the fire. I turned my head. It was Chil-sing's cool hand on my neck. He was helping me up.

Tears streamed from my eyes. I hadn't cried since I was a small boy. Now the tears poured, silently, steadily in streams down my cheeks. As I stood there, Augustine reached out her hand to my cheek. She touched the tears there, then moved her hand down my neck, my shoulder, down the side of my body to my feet. Chil-sing reached out to the other side of my face and did the same, bowing down before me in a motion like washing down the side of my body.

The people got up from their seats on the steps. One by one, they came up to me, touched my tears, and moved their hands across my body, washing me with my own tears. My tears poured out faster as I understood that I was undergoing a ceremony of purification and forgiveness. They touched me, one by one. Some of them were crying too. Then each turned, walked up the steps, and left.

Chil-sing and the other young ones who had made up my "gang" waited till the last. Then, at a nod from Augustine, they went down on their knees and said, in unison, "Forgive us for wanting to hit you."

I choked a couple of times before I had enough control to answer. "Forgive me," was all I could manage. The young ones reached forward to touch my tears, then made motions of cleansing themselves with them as they climbed up the steps.

Then I was alone with the people of my ka. They helped me back to the ka and laid me down as one of the spokes of the sleeping wheel. There were eleven of us now.

"Nagdeo," everyone whispered.

"Nagdeo," I said, and fell asleep.

Three

The next morning I awoke first, while it was still dark. I surveyed our sleeping wheel with its gap where the old Frenchman had lain. Moving clockwise from me was first Augustine, then Chil-sing, Next came Aya and Salvatore, then the Greek-looking redhead who had no name. I had learned that few of the people had a name until they were about thirty, when they chose their own name, or, as they would express it, a name came to them in their dreams. Chil-sing was unusual in having a name before he had reached manhood.

And Jamal, the seven year old who lay opposite me in the sleeping wheel, was truly precocious in having a name already at his age. Next to him lay the Indian-looking girl, then a gap where the old Frenchman had lain, then the little three year old, then huge Sbgai. Next to me lay Doe, now the oldest of our "family." Doe seldom left the village, but tended the plants near the stone walls.

As I lay watching, people began to stir. I got rather

shakily to my feet as I was approached by Jamal, who took off his blanket and stood naked before me. We reached toward the top of the ka, spread our arms wide, then made our palms meet in front of our chests.

"I have fruit," Jamal began. "Seven pieces of fruit." He spread his fingers to show how many. "I give my fruit to Salvatore, and my fruit grows large, like the moon. It goes up and up till it is far away, shining in the sky, seven moons."

I stood still, waiting for him to go on, but he did not. I cleared my throat and began. "I . . . " I began three times before I was finally able to speak to the little boy, who kept his hands clasped before him and did not move except to scratch one big toe with the other one. "I am in a very dark place. But the dark is full of shadows. The shadows move and swell. They are all around me, and I am afraid." I concentrated, trying to remember. "They snatch at me. They grab my tunic. I spin round and round trying to keep them off me. My tunic is torn off. I am naked. Then I see a hol-ka. I dive into the opening, and crawl into the dark hol-ka. But I cannot close the hol-ka. I know the shadows will follow me into the hol-ka, and they will come and press against me; they will touch me, and I will no longer be able to run away."

The boy made a little bow to me. The others were still murmuring their dreams, as we walked out, but I saw some of them beginning to follow after us. We walked the spiral outward together, and I asked Jamal, "Why do we tell each other our dreams in the morning?"

He looked at me as if I had asked a very obvious question. "Why," he said, "so we will not forget, of course. If you do not tell a dream right away, it slips away from you."

"That's true," I agreed. "But why don't we write them down?"

His confused look confirmed what I had already observed: there was no knowledge of graphic representation, either pictures or writing.

When we reached the end of the spiral, I started off into the field, expecting to join some of the poeple who were moving toward the orchards, where they had been harvesting fruit for the past two days. I felt someone tug at my tunic.

"What is it, Jamal?"

The boy looked at me, puzzled. "But you are going into a hol-ka," he said.

"What?"

"Try to pick the one you saw in your dreams. Which one was it?"

"No special one."

The boy waited. "Aren't you going in?"

"You mean because my dream tells me to."

"Yes," said the boy.

"Do you always do what your dreams tell you?"

"Always," said the boy. "If I am sure. If the dream is clear."

"And you think my dream was clear?"

"Very clear," he said, and stood before me expectantly.

His steady gaze was too much. After hesitating for a moment, I pulled off my tunic, folded it and placed it on the ground, then got down on my hands and knees. I took one more look at the boy's now smiling face before I crawled inside.

I crawled inward in the dark, slipping downward into

the depths of the mound. I came to rest on a mat. I could see nothing at all. I sat up, crosslegged. I could see nothing, hear nothing. I only sensed the nearness of the stone walls, the stone and clay roof over my head, that I could touch by simply raising one arm.

A horrible, sick fear uncoiled itself like a snake in my belly. I could hear my breathing, short rasping gasps. I jumped up and hit my head on the stones above. I sat down again. My flesh crawled. I imagined all kinds of repulsive vermin crawling out of the walls and covering me. Twice I headed for the tunnel and began to crawl out, but I stopped myself and went back.

I began to feel that I might suffocate. I gasped for breath, panted. I broke out in a sweat of apprehension that the stone roof would fall in on me and bury me alive. I was already buried alive, entombed.

In that first session in the hol-ka, that was all that happened. I had no idea how long I stayed. For hours, it seemed, I drifted through alternate states of terror. Fears washed over me like waves: fear of dying, fear of being buried, fear of not finding the way out, fear of being squeezed to death by black shadows, fear of everything. I sweated and panted my fear out, until there was no more fear. Just numbness. I felt nothing. The terror had oozed out of my pores. I was empty.

I crawled out, put on my tunic and sat blinking at the sun. It was in the same place in the sky. Not more than about twenty minutes could have gone by. I rested for a few minutes, and although I had come out of the hol-ka panting and exhausted, I began to feel fresh and invigorated, as I used to after a brisk swim.

I crossed the fields to where people were picking the ripe fruit off the trees. I watched them fill the fronts of their tunics with a variety of fruit from the different kinds of trees all growing together. Then they walked through the orchard toward the hill. I followed. They climbed a few steps up the side of the hill, stopping at the first outcropping of rock. On the level surfaces of rock they laid out the fruit to dry. Small children stood near each rock, waving away the birds that came to sample the fruit. "Yours is at the top of the tree," each child would say as he waved away the birds, most of which were tame and unafraid.

"May I help?"

The nearest person simply nodded at me, and I remembered that the Ata people did not like to talk overmuch.

I ran down the hill, found a tree where no one was working, and filled the front of my tunic, holding it up like an apron. Then I climbed back up to a rock, and covered all the level surfaces. As soon as I had finished, I hurried back down again.

After about five trips, I began to feel tired, but I pushed on. On the sixth trip I stumbled and spilled most of the plums. The sun was very hot, and when I went to pick up the plums, I came up dizzy. I also came up looking into the face of Sbgai, the hairy giant whose gruff voice I had so far heard only in the morning as he recited his dreams. He sat down on the side of the hill, and motioned for me to do so. I sat down beside him. He bit into a plum and handed me one. For a few minutes we ate in silence. Biting into the plum made me realize how dry my mouth was.

"To work too hard is donagdeo; it will give you sore

muscles and a headache. And all night you will dream of dogs biting your legs or of trees falling on your aching back." He laughed.

"But you work very hard," I told him. "I have watched you. Sometimes you stay in the fields all day."

"But with a body like this," he said, throwing out his arms as though to display something comical, "I must work hard, or I would have fretful dreams, dreams of weeping kin and mean sayings."

"How much should I work?"

"However much makes your body ready for good dreams. At first, now, not too much, I think. It will change. Later you will work more. You will find the rhythm. No work makes mean dreams; too much work makes pain and twitching. Useless dreams either way. You understand?"

I nodded. "But I'm not sure I'll know how much is enough. I'm so unused to physical labor that . . . "

" Your body will find out. Let your body tell you." Sbgai got up and stretched. "This body carries me off now, to move and move." He grinned at me, then turned and stomped off down the hill.

I sat and watched him for a while. I still believed that letting their dreams rule their waking life was superstitious and would stifle any progress for the people of Ata. But I had to admit that this simple self-regulating manner of deciding how much work to do was not only practical—it was almost ingenious. For, assuming all the people truly believed in their dreams, and lived with only one ambition, to be "strong dreamers," the ordering of work in this little society was assured without compulsion.

No one would exhaust himself in compulsive work, lest he be restricted to dreaming only of "trees falling on his aching back." But more important, no one would want to exist entirely on the labor of others, lest he dream "mean" dreams.

I slowed down, moving with the swinging rhythm of the others and stopping frequently to take a drink from the skin brought around by one of the children. Still it was hard work, and the hours passed slowly. I could have gone back to the village at any time, but I was ashamed to leave. I saw some of the people lie down in the shade and close their eyes from time to time, and I did the same. Then in the late afternoon, I seemed to discover a kind of rhythm of work, and for a time I moved without conscious thought, as though I were a marionette, my movements achieved by the pulling of invisible strings, with no effort to me. This lasted for an hour, perhaps two (I was already becoming unsure of time) and then I lost the rhythm, pulled against the strings, and realized how tired I was.

By then it was sunset and we all began walking back toward the village. I was tempted to run, if I could have, because I was so hungry. During the day, I could have eaten more fruit while I worked, but I noticed that only children and nursing mothers ate while they worked. Most adults took nothing but water.

I tried not to think of food. The procession inward was slow and interrupted with much singing, and occasional dances by the young ones, watched indulgently by the older ones. By the time we reached the pool I felt more relaxed, if still hungry, and the little sprinkle of water was refreshing.

I walked straight down the steps of the la-ka and reached for one of the pots near the fire. It was the usual simple stew that some of the people had spent the afternoon preparing, delicately scented with herbs and barely cooked in the clay pots which sat near the fire. There were only twelve pots, and I felt as if I could have eaten one of them by myself. Of course, there were plenty of leaves and fruit on all the steps, but I wanted something hot and substantial. I could not resist reaching into the pot and feeding myself five or six handfuls. No one stopped me, but I was immediately surrounded by people with pots, offering me bits from their fingers. I was being indulged, like a greedy child. I felt a flash of embarrassed anger, but the people were obviously of such good, simple nature that it would be ridiculous, even more childish, to be angry. I let myself be fed from their hands, then fed the remains of the pot I held to the oldsters sitting on the steps nearest the fire.

When everyone had finished eating, we sat down as usual. I would much rather have gone back to the ka and gone to sleep, but I conformed. I had made myself a promise. After all the trouble I had caused here, the least I could do was to conform to the life of the people until next spring when they would be able to get me off the island. The others were leaning forward expectantly.

This time it was Aya, her pale, gray-streaked hair flowing over the white kitten on her shoulder. She told the Grass Story, one of the favorites of Ata, which could be done with many variations.

Basically the story was very simple, in its general pattern, describing short blades of grass as the first life on

Ata. These, so the story went, were swept away by tidal waves. The grass sprouted up again and was blown away by winds. It sprouted again and was scorched by the sun. And so on.

While Aya told the story, some of the children got up and began to pantomime it, the smallest one acting the part of a blade of grass that continually popped up again after some form of destruction acted out by five or six other children. It became very funny to see the toddling four year old pop up grinning after every defeat by elements, animals and men. I forgot my weariness and my aches and pains; or perhaps laughing with the other people took them away.

But when the story and pantomime were over, everyone stood very solemnly for the triple "Nagdeo," before they left. On the way back to our ka I asked Chil-sing why the mood had dropped to such seriousness, after such a lighthearted story.

"You found it lighthearted?"

"Well, I suppose there were serious undertones."

"Always serious," he said, "when we enter the presence of the dream." I could see from the look on his face that he hoped I would not force him to talk anymore. We fell asleep, and there were no shadows in my dream that night.

The next morning it was Chil-sing who faced me to tell his dreams. He frowned as he recited a series of fragments, images that did not fit together but repeated themselves in a circle, like the spun wheel of pictures. When he was through I smiled and began, "I dreamed of a great table and on the table were cakes and pies, red meat, a great mound of chocolate . . . " He waited politely until I was through, and then we set off together for the fields.

"I dreamed of eating," I said. "That's not very strong dreaming, is it?"

"Depends on what it means," said Chil-sing.

"Look, all it means is that I'm hungry. I'm hungry all the time. I'm a pretty jaded person, you know, used to many rich foods, so I dream of them at night."

"If it means only that, it will soon disappear."

"I doubt it. I'm surprised you don't all dream of eating all the time. You all eat so little."

"Too much food is donagdeo."

"And by your methods you can't produce a lot anyway. It has to be strictly rationed, right?"

"I do not know. It takes little food to sustain a body. But food becomes more when it is given, not taken."

"What do you mean?"

"It is one of the old dreams. You have not heard it yet?"

"No."

"Once, long ago, when Ata was very young and the twelve times twelve people had not yet dug and built the great la-ka, but sat to tell dreams beneath the branches of the great Life Tree, a strong dreamer, a waking-dreamer, was born among them. He had been born as a baby, torn out of the body, long before, but then he was born again as a waking-dreamer. And all this happened in the midst of famine, when the harvest of summer was gone, and the root crop of fall had been dug up, and still the winter fast had long to go before the first new grass would come to feed the people." He recited in a rhythmic style that indicated he had heard the story many times.

"And the waking-dreamer sat beneath the Life Tree and the people all came before him, and they said, 'We have only these twelve pots of grain left and these twelve baskets of fruit. Some will eat and some will starve. Tell us who shall live and who shall die before those of us who are strong take all, and the people of Ata is reduced to strong bodies with bad dreams.'

"And the waking-dreamer said, 'You feed all the people.' But the people protested and said, 'We have not enough for all the people.'

"'You have not enough for yourselves,' said the waking-dreamer. 'If you feed yourselves you will starve, but each feed another, and all will be filled, for kin are nourished by what they feed to others.'

"And so twelve people picked up twelve pots and began to feed others from the pots. And twelve more picked up twelve baskets of fruit and began to feed all the twelve times twelve people from the baskets. And when they were through, and all were fed, all having been fed from the hands of others, the pots and the baskets were still full and so were the people."

We walked on in silence. "That's a very nice story," I said.

"It is truth," said Chil-sing. "It is one of the great dreams of our people."

"And because of that story—that dream—you feed one another."

"And there is always enough," said Chil-sing.

"Perhaps because you believe there is." He didn't answer. "There is a story like that one set down long ago in the outside world." I proceeded with a very halting, stumbling and mixed up version of the loaves and fishes, and Chil-sing listened with great interest.

When I finished he said, "Yes, that is a corrupt version of our dream."

I was a little taken aback by the arrogance of the statement. "What do you mean? In the outside world, that story is part of a great literature of people advanced enough to make markings that speak, instead of having to repeat stories night after night before a fire."

"That may be," said Chil-sing, "but the point of the dream is lost. The waking-dreamer of your story is just a trickster who can make many fishes from a few. It is not his act, but the act of the people in feeding one another that multiplies the food. Such a story becomes donagdeo when it is so corrupted. Perhaps if your people had not put it down into markings, they could have improved it, dreaming it over until it got better, instead of being stuck in such a meaningless story."

I had to admit that I too had found it meaningless. "What is a waking-dreamer?"

"Just what the name says. One who lives in the dream all the time, asleep or awake. One who goes Home without dying."

"Are there many here?"

"None." He looked at me and laughed. "You ask as if a waking-dreamer is born every day." Then he shook his head to show me that he didn't want to talk anymore.

I began to look at the people walking before and behind me. They looked perfectly healthy for a race living on what seemed to me to be inadequate food, and doing heavy work. There were no fat ones, of course. They were a lean group, for all their differences of color and stature. But none was emaciated, and the children were as plump and active as any I had ever seen.

We had reached the circle of hol-ka, and something made me stop. Chil-sing went on without me. I looked at the hol-ka and felt a slight chill, and then I remembered that while I had dreamed of cake and steak the night before, at least the nightmares were gone. If there was any connection between that and my brief session in the hol-ka yesterday, it was worth trying again. Perhaps I sweated out my nightmares there, and could be free of them at night—if only free to dream of childish trivia.

I pulled off my tunic and crawled into the hol-ka. My experience was much the same as the day before, if anything, worse. The agony of fear and panic seemed longer, and just as I thought it would last forever, it let go of me, dropped me, shaking and sweating. I crawled out and went to work.

Things went on this way for a while, and I would have been content except for one thing. Augustine seemed to be avoiding me. If I went to work near her, she moved away. In the la-ka at night she managed to sit always on the side opposite mine, with the fire and the dream-teller between us. And, although we slept together in the same sleeping wheel at night, there was no place where people were more alone, more on their own, than during those nightly journeys into the dreams that were believed to be reality.

I began to believe that, despite her act in the la-ka, she could not forgive me for killing the old man. I knew she

105

must be involved in some inner struggle, because she spent so much time in the hol-ka. Every day she returned to one for longer and longer sessions, which no one else seemed to notice, and one night she did not come out at all, leaving a gap in our sleeping wheel as she had the night after I attacked her.

On the next Bath Day I got up, recited my dream of climbing the Life Tree to get a roast pig that sat on the topmost branch (I never got there in the dream) and we all started off to the beach.

I knew the ritual pretty well. We walked to the edge of the waves, threw our flowers into the water, then took off our tunics, joined hands and walked forward into the water. Everyone kept his eyes on the sun rising out of the water in front of us. But I was still unable to resist taking a quick look at some of the girls' bodies. Since I didn't bother any of them, I thought that this bit of peeking was harmless.

As I was looking to my right, I felt my left hand being released, then grasped again by a different hand. Someone had broken into the line, but that fact was of little interest to me. Only when we were shoulder deep in the water and had dropped all solemnity to turn and playfully wash one another, did I see, as I turned to my left, that I had been holding hands with Augustine.

She did not smile as she cupped her hands, picked up water and poured it over my head. I did the same to her. Then I loosened her hair from its braid. She turned her back on me and let her head fall backward. I washed her hair in the water. Her eyes were closed. When she opened them again, she was smiling, and she splashed some water into my face. I splashed her back, and we laughed and played along with the children.

When we started to walk back through the water, she took my hand again. We did not look at each other as we each put on our tunic. Again she took my hand and led me across the sand to where the river emptied into the sea. We followed the river upstream, until we came to a grassy bank with trees.

She turned to face me.

"I am to be woman to you," she said simply, without any expression.

For a minute I stood there stupidly. Then I untied and took off her tunic. She sat down while I pulled mine off. She smiled once as I laid her back against the grassy slope.

Our love-making was a kind of ceremony, like a stamp or a seal upon something. I entered her almost immediately, and as I felt myself coming, I heard a low crooning sigh from her that told me she was with me. Then we lay together on our side, her arms and legs enveloping me, our eyes looking straight into one another's. We did not talk at all. This was a ritual to cancel out the rape, a purified re-enactment.

"What made you change your mind?" Before she spoke, I knew what her answer would be.

"After you came back to us, the dream began. Every night, all night."

"What was the dream?"

"You were on your knees before me saying that you could not live without me."

That wasn't exactly what I wanted to hear. "And nothing about your own needs?" She didn't answer me.

"Okay, if I was begging for you, why did you keep trying to hold out? I thought you always followed your dreams without question."

Her skin deepened slightly and her eyes shifted once before they came back to mine. "I was selfish. Self-willed. But you're right. I should not fight against the dream."

"Selfish?"

"I had hoped it was over. I had hoped I was through with it. It is donagdeo to be so ambitious, self-defeating, of course. But I thought . . . "

"Through with what?"

"With being woman to a man."

I laughed. "You hoped you were through with sex?" She nodded, and I laughed again. "Don't try to tell me you don't enjoy sex!"

"I do."

"Then what's wrong with it?" I shook my head as I looked at her. The same old problem. The same old guilt. The same sex-ridden, sex-fearing ghosts haunted these people as haunted everyone outside.

"It takes too much. It is . . . "

"Donagdeo? Come on, I can't dream of anything but sex when I can't have any—like food."

She was shaking her head. "Yes, like food. But not like food. Higher and greater than food. You do not take sex as seriously as . . . "

"I assure you, I do," I said, kissing the tip of her nose.

" . . . we who know it stands for the greater dream. And to reach it . . . "

" . . . you try to give up sex?"

"No. We let it give us up. So that it can become something that sets us free to . . . "

"To what?"

"I do not know. I am not yet free, it seems." And she gave a little chuckle along with a quick squeeze of her legs around me.

Somehow that playful squeeze touched me deeply. I felt that I had entered upon some kind of commitment. Before, I had believed that relations with women were impossible without lies. But this time, looking into Augustine's eyes, I felt that this relationship would be impossible without truth.

"You understand that I am leaving in the spring."

"Yes."

"You can forget me?"

"Why should I?"

"Because I'll leave nothing behind but . . . "

"You will leave a child behind."

"You're pregnant?"

"Yes."

We sat quietly for a minute. "I'm sorry . . . sorry it happened that way." But she only shrugged. "So that is why you decided . . . " I had to ask her for the possessive "my"; the word was rarely used. " . . . that you are my woman."

Her eyes flashed. "I am not your woman. No one belongs to anyone. I said I would be woman to you. Why should I say that because I am pregnant? I do not belong to the man who fathered my other one."

"You have a child. Which one?" She described a big, swarthy adolescent boy I'd seen in the la-ka. "Why don't you live with him, with his father?"

"I live with them. We all live together here, don't we? But he is not my boy and his father not my man. No one belongs to anyone else."

"You belong to yourself. That's good."

She recoiled in shock. "Oh, no. No."

"Then who do you belong to?" She only smiled. "How old are you?" I asked, but she did not understand the concept of measuring age by years. I could not tell her age, but guessed she must be older than I, by the age of her son, though she did not look older. "Were you very young when you had your child?" She nodded.

We made love again, more slowly this time. I had meant to give her great pleasure, but I began to fumble nervously like a boy, to feel foolish and stupid. It was her steady eyes on me, her total and open acceptance of me, her quiet pleasuring in my touch of her that ruined it for me that time. She was not an adversary, nor was she simply a body to be aroused by prescribed techniques to prescribed responses. I was not fucking her. And I was afraid.

Several times we turned away from each other as if to give up. Then she came close to me again, kissed my neck or my cheek and drew me on. The third time, I sat up, feeling myself in danger of losing some kind of struggle, losing because there was no struggle.

She got up and sat on my lap, facing me, working my organ into her, like a lever on which she would fasten herself to me. Then she put her arms around my neck, lay her head on my shoulder, like a tired child, and was still. Then gently, instinctively, like a loving father, I rocked her, until the heat rose in us both in a smooth, quiet wave, spilling over us together.

Face to face we looked at each other again, and I said, "I will be man to you."

I meant it too, but my attempts to prove it got no-where. I wanted to build a ka for the two of us, apart from the others, as man and wife should live, I told her. But she seemed horrified at the idea that the two of us should leave the ka to live alone. "We can perhaps move to another ka if this sleeping wheel does not help your dreams." I told her I wanted us to be alone so that we could make love anytime we wanted to, but she said we could make love any time we wanted to as things were, except during the night which was reserved for sleep. Then she said, "Before long, we will not want to make love so much. Then if we lived alone, we should have nothing but each other. Two is the number for making love. Two is a very strong number; for other things it is too strong."

"Donagdeo?" She nodded. "Twelve is the magic number here, is that it?"

"For the ka, for sleeping together, yes, especially dur-ing the winter fast. But all numbers are 'magic' for differ-ent things."

"For what?"

She told me that in a few days the young kin would repeat the dance of numbers in the la-ka, and that after I learned the dance, I would understand.

"Will the dance be done with the ornaments? The precious stones, the gold crown?"

She took a long time to answer. "If that is what you want," she finally answered.

"What do you mean?"

"I do not see such things in the dances or the dreams. If you see them, they are there, they are true, for you."

"You mean they're all in my head. I was hypnotized.

They don't really exist."

"Yes, they exist." Then she saw that we meant something different. "In this way," she pinched my arm, "they do not exist. When we watch the dance, when we listen to the dreams, we are in the presence of what is most real and most precious. But we cannot see it or touch it, and so, perhaps it appears to each of us in the forms of that which we treasure. For you, because in the great world, these stones are valued . . . "

"I hallucinated rubies," I grunted disgustedly.

"You saw that something presented before you, something which you could not understand, was a great treasure."

I told her that I had seen the old Frenchman after his death, and she said that meant I was potentially a strong dreamer. "Yes," I told her, "I dream of apple pie and bogeymen." She refused to laugh and said that to see things while awake was very advanced. I answered that in the great world, we lock up people who see things while awake, and when I laughed, she looked sad.

"Maybe I'm a medium," I said, jokingly, to try to cheer her up. "I can call back the dead. Anyone you want to see?"

But she became even more serious. "You would not want to do that, to keep them from Home. Tam came to you after his death because he did not want you to go on suffering. But you would not want him to delay any longer."

On the night before next Bath Day I watched the dance of numbers for the first time. I watched it many times after that, and learned to participate in it myself, since the kin of Ata placed great importance on everyone learning and participating in the dances, especially the dance of numbers, until they were too old for such strenuous expression. The dance was performed in the la-ka around and in the central fire pit after the fire had died to ashes which were stirred until cooled.

The dancers performed nude and carried lighted torches strapped to both wrists, so that their bodies were seen as wicks to a double candle flame, flickering and moving in the darkness. Twelve was always the starting number for the dance.

The twelve stood around the pit, facing inward, with their hands together in front of their faces, as if looking at each other through the single flame made by their two torches. They clapped their hands three times, making sparks fly, then formed a square, with three on each side, facing each other across the pit. Then they clapped their hands four times and formed a triangle, with four on each side; another clap and they were pairs facing one another; yet another and they were a circle again, holding hands and joining their flames as they moved slowly around the pit. They did this twelve times.

The first time I saw it, I thought the movements monotonous. It was a long time before I learned to appreciate the increasing beauty of the repetition, the deeper harmony of the moving together as they caught the rhythm and moved with it. And, of course, only when I had actually done the dance myself did I begin to appreciate the power of this repetition.

At the end of this sequence one of the dancers jumped

into the pit and crouched unseen except for the faint glow of his torches.

Then four of the dancers faced each other at points north, south, east and west of the pit. They stood quite still, their hands clasped over their heads, their torches flaming upward. The other seven became frantic, running and jumping around and among the four, waving their arms and throwing fiery sparks everywhere, taking wild, running leaps across the pit. The four standing dancers never moved. This phase of the dance continued until one of the leapers, through misjudgment or fatigue, did not quite clear the pit; he or she would then crouch down in the pit with the other one.

At this point the dance became as dignified as it had been frenzied. The ten dancers sat down with their backs to the pit and their knees bent up to their chests. They bowed their heads to their knees and thrust their arms forward, so that those watching saw nothing but their hands with flames seeming to rise from the fingers.

This phase of the dance was performed entirely by the fingers, forming intricate mathematical combinations which I never learned to do with any ease. The combinations were never the same twice and the subtlety of movement of the one hundred fingers of the ten dancers had an uncanny, hypnotic effect, so that all was absolutely still by the time one more dancer rolled over backward into the pit.

In the deep hush that followed, the remaining nine dancers stood up and broke off into three groups of three. In each group the three dancers faced each other, clasped their hands together into one blazing torch, and went round in a circle three times. Then all three groups leaped to the edge of the pit, reaching their arms as far inward as they could without falling into the pit, trying to touch all their flames into one central flame above the center of the pit. They circled the pit three times, then went back to their three groups of three. This was repeated until, in the leaning forward over the pit, one of the dancers lost his balance and fell in. This part of the dance was always accompanied by a quick stomping of feet by the watchers, so that a low, dampened and ominous thunder resounded throughout.

The eight remaining dancers formed two squares, one cutting through the other, put their arms out to their sides to join torches, then, facing outward from the pit, slowly circled it, each dancer forming the point of an eight-pointed star. In this part of the dance there was some laughing and jostling, until one of the dancers was pushed into the pit, amidst general laughter.

The relaxed mood continued, as four of the remaining seven dancers took the north-south-east-west positions. The other three dancers formed a triangle which moved from one to another of the four compass points, circling each of them three times in gentle, even reverent movements, until one of the triangle jumped into the pit.

The two left turned the dance into a game of tag, in which they dodged around each of the four compass points, which never moved . . . until finally one caught the other and threw him into the pit.

The one that was left became a clown, harassing the four compass points, acting out every possible means to trip, push, jar, frighten, somehow plunge one of the four stationary dancers into the pit. But the four remained still and unmovable as, amid delighted laughter, the clown grew more and more frantic in his or her attempts to unbalance one of them. Finally with a cry of mock frustration, the clown jumped into the pit.

The four remained quite still until the laughter died to complete silence. Then another few moments of stillness.

Then all four of them stepped down into the pit, where by this time there was a mound of huddled bodies. One of the four (usually south) joined the mound. The other three climbed upon it. One of them climbed onto the mound of crouched dancers on his hands and knees and stayed that way, firmly clutching the mound and looking down upon it. The next climbed onto him and straddled his back, looking straight ahead, then from side to side, thrusting his torches before him as if to see where he was going. The third climbed onto the shoulders of this one and stood reaching upward, stretching and straining, toward the point where the tree-trunk frame of the la-ka joined high above.

During this part of the dance there was singing from the spectators, which reached higher and higher pitches each time the standing dancer strained upward.

When the singing ended, the dancer on his hands and knees melted into the mound, while the other two jumped out of the pit again and faced each other across it.

This part of the dance was almost ferocious, as the two opposites traded act for act. Usually the two were a man and a woman, and this part of the dance was improvised in hundreds of different ways. Only one thing remained consistent; for every move made by one dancer, an opposing move was made simultaneously by the other. Utter concentration on the intent of the opposing partner in the dance was necessary, as I learned much later when I tried

116

it, and the leading role was never in the control of one for long. The pace of this dance speeded up imperceptibly; faster and faster the two opposing partners moved until suddenly both threw themselves forward into the pit and, clasping one another close, fell as one upon the mound.

There was a deep silence for about five minutes. Then slowly we saw the glow of all the torches rise up above the rim of the pit. Slowly, very slowly, a single one of the dancers rose, in the center of the pit, as if out of the flames of the held torches. The dancer rose and stood, naked and without torches, arms outstretched to the sides, body glowing in the light of the torches.

A great sigh swept over all the people in the la-ka, and the dance was over.

Afterward I asked Augustine the meaning of the dance.

"It is itself," she said.

"But movements have meanings. I'm asking you to interpret the meanings of those movements. There must be a great meaning for your people behind those movements.

"Yes."

"What is it?"

"I do not know." She looked a little worried, a little distant from me. "Why do you look so uneasy? Is it because you are hiding something from me?"

"No." She looked so much more worried now that I had to believe her. "Of course, the movements have meanings behind them. If we were sure of the meanings, we would not need the dance. There is a great danger in trying to interpret the dance in words. Words get between us and the dance and the meaning behind the dance—just one more thing between us and the meaning. One must dance the dance and go through it to the meaning."

We got off into a discussion of the Ata language, one of many I had with her. It seemed that the word for word was the same as the word for false or lie. And the language was amazingly concrete. It contained few abstractions except nagdeo and donagdeo. There were words for good or bad, honor or duty, and other lofty concepts. But they were seldom used. And there was no word for happiness. Nagdeo encompassed all that was positive, and donagdeo, all that was negative. These two terms were never applied to persons, only to acts. Persons were just kin, neutral, neuter, unmodified.

The conversation ended when Augustine asked me to define happiness. I began to fumble with the word. Then I used the phrase "pursuit of happiness" and became even more confused when she remarked that it did not seem that what I described as happiness could be gained by pursuit. When I reached the point of embarrassed confusion, she did not laugh. She only repeated, "That is the trouble with words."

"But you people use words constantly to describe your dreams."

"Yes, that is the best way we know. Except dance and music. They are better."

"But you use words only to describe things, not concepts, not meaning behind the things."

"Yes," she would agree, and we would be back in the same circular discussion, until she would beg me please to stop making her talk.

There was a more serious problem in our relationship. She acceded to my every wish. She was always affectionate. Our lovemaking was frequent, and it got better and better. Yet I felt there was a great distance between us. One day I said to her, "You are willing when I want to make love, but you never come to me and ask." After that she frequently initiated our lovemaking. But still I wasn't satisfied. She enjoyed our lovemaking and was remarkably passionate, but even at the moment of orgasm I never felt I possessed her completely. I often accused her of not loving me, and as I explained what I meant by love, she became silent and serious, making no attempt to reassure me that she did love me.

After questioning and calculating, I decided she was only a couple of years older than I. Her lean, unlined face looked younger, but in her actions she seemed hundreds of years old. Once when I was complaining, she patted me, as she would in order to soothe an irritable child, and I nearly hit her. I stopped my hand in time and went into a hol-ka to cool off. That night I had a peculiar dream.

I was back in the world, with a woman—an anonymous one, like the women I always had, blonde, twenty, with sharp discontented eyes. We were arguing, and she was pouting and gesticulating and saying, "You don't love me." Prancing back and forth, naked, on a runway of the sort found in old burlesque houses, she poured out all of the words I'd used against Augustine. As she pranced she shrank and grew younger until she was a whining infant. I began to laugh at her, and then I woke up.

That morning I wanted to tell my dream to Augustine but she was already occupied with Jamal, so I told it, with some embarrassment, to Salvatore, who heard it with apparent indifference. I wanted to tell the dream, discuss it, interpret it, but during the whole day there was no chance. But the next time I began to complain to Augustine, I saw the whining female of my dream, and my words were too funny to continue. I stopped demanding Augustine's dependence. And the moment I did her passion and joy in our lovemaking seemed to double, and there were weeks of full, almost delerious lovemaking nearly every day in the grove by the river where we had first come together.

Meanwhile Augustine's belly was rounding, and the days were getting shorter. We spent less time in the fields now and more time preparing food for storage. Gradually the steps of the la-ka were filled with more and more dried fruits, wrapped bundles of grain, legumes, and nuts, until it became hard to find a place to sit for the evening stories. The fields were planted in root vegetables, which would be left in the ground until we exhausted the stores in the la-ka.

We began to spend most afternoons sitting in the sun and weaving mats. The mats were used to cover the great framework of the la-ka and were completed just in time, only three days before the first fall rain. Other mats were used to mend the coverings over the separate kas. Sometimes we wove the mats in silence, or someone would begin a song or tell one of the old stories. There was an unending supply of stories.

"Is the winter hard?" I asked Augustine.

She laughed, and the pink butterfly that hovered next to her ear rose to circle her head. "The winter is given entirely to dreaming. It is a wonderful time."

"And the winter fast that Salvatore mentioned?"

"That will come when there is food enough left only for the young and the old."

"And the pregnant?"

"Yes," she agreed, smiling.

"We should have planted more and stored it in the hol-kas."

"The hol-kas are unusable, damp in the winter. Even the la-ka's fire pit sometimes becomes a small pool."

"Do we go to the la-ka to eat in the winter?"

"No, only to bring food back to the ka."

"And when the food is gone?"

"We dig up the roots."

"And when the roots are gone?"

"We fast until the first grass."

"What if there is not enough?"

"There is enough. There is always enough. If we dream well, there will be enough food."

In effect then, we were preparing for a kind of hibernation. On the day that the la-ka was completely filled and there was no more room to sit, the leaves began to fall from the Life Tree.

The people gathered that day under the Life Tree, sitting under it as the wind blew the leaves down upon them. They gathered up the dry leaves and brought them to the kas. Other leaves were swept up and soon the kas were almost knee deep in warm, dry leaves. Every day the weaving continued, and every day the people gathered under the tree, until all the leaves were gone.

There were still many fine days left, but we all spent more time in the kas. Sleeping periods extended to fill the longer nights, and I often found myself sitting up alone in the dark, long before sunup, waiting for the others to awaken. They had worked hard during the long days, and now they slept just as long and just as hard. Their movements slowed and there was no more dancing. They were conserving energy.

As it grew colder, we began to bring the animals into the ka at night. One night, when I had begun to shiver even before it was quite dark, a small brown she-goat with a dark face put its face into the ka between two mats that had loosened. The goat came in. I got up to fasten the mats, and when I returned to my place, I found the goat sitting there. I stretched out my back against it, and it kept me warm. In the morning it followed me outside and after that was never far from my side.

"Your animal has found you," said Augustine. "That is nagdeo."

"And she'll keep me warmer this winter than your butterflies will."

She smiled and looked at the gray moth clinging in stillness to her shoulder. "Soon even these will be gone."

Tenderness for her filled me, surprising me with its intensity. I insisted that the goat sleep between us and often pushed it toward her in the depths of the cold nights. Sometimes, when I did so, she would smile in her sleep and hug the goat to her belly. The people stopped gathering at the Life Tree each night and we took up a different routine. When the gray light of dawn came, we stood and told our dreams. Then we went out to relieve ourselves and to wash. We cleaned out the ka every morning, sifting through the leaves for animal droppings, shaking out our sleeping mats. Then, leaving the old and the very young in the ka, we went out on inspection tour of the village, repairing holes ripped in mat roofs by wind (which became increasingly strong and cold), refilling the water skins and pots. Last we went to the la-ka, checked the stores and made necessary repairs. We set out some food for the animals, then gathered rations for the people in our ka.

Back in the ka, we fed each other as we would have in the la-ka. Then we sat in a circle, with our animals among us, and told stories.

People took turns telling the stories, one person each day. The story of that person would go on for hours, with the storyteller resting at regular intervals while the others sang or chanted. Listeners could interrupt the story at any time to ask a question and even, sometimes, to offer a suggestion for the plot. I began to enjoy these winter tales more than I had the ritualistic tales of the la-ka, and I wish I had time to write down some of them. One day I asked Chil-sing if the stories were traditional ones of the island.

"No," he told me. "Each is our own story, made up from our own dreams and from our waking too."

"They are not spontaneous."

"No." Chil-sing smiled. "We save them, we harvest them, we store them as we store food for the winter and we feed our kin on stories. The stories and dances of the la-ka come partly from our winter tales too; those that are repeated by request, winter after winter, are shared by all in the la-ka eventually."

These stories went on until darkness came and everyone settled down to dream his own stories.

As the periods of darkness grew longer, I suffered horribly. I could not sleep as long as the others, and I could not seem to get warm enough. I was hungry all the time, though I imagine that my main problem was boredom, as I lay awake in the dark listening to the others breathe.

I was grateful for the heavy rains that came. They gave me work to do, mending leaks in our ka and others, wading out through the village (the ka stayed quite dry, but the paths ran like rivers). And during the long, dark hours in the ka, the sound of the rain, gentle and steady on the matted walls of the ka, helped me to doze.

One day Salvatore asked if I would take my turn at story telling.

"I have prepared nothing for the winter tales," I said.

He shrugged and said, "There is your whole life —preparation enough. We are hungry for stories." I found it hard to refuse such a request, and when we sat down after eating, I began.

I had intended simply to tell something of my childhood. I found myself remembering happenings I hadn't thought of for years. I described a house that I had left when I was not more than two years old. It was as if I too were listening to a story I had never heard before.

After that first experience I took my turn every few days and told an episode from my life. I tried to choose the more important, more dramatic episodes, but they all sounded dull and contrived next to the winter tales of the others, even of the children like Jamal. After a while I fell back on impressions and daydreams of my childhood, stories of a boy who had ceased to exist until resurrected in that circle in a dark tent that smelled of goat.

Darkness lengthened and deepened. The winds were sharp and rains frequent. The children hardly woke from sleep anymore except to eat what was brought and fed into their mouths. The old sat up from time to time, but hardly spoke. I began to notice that when Salvatore, Sbgai, Augustine and Doe (our oldest) were not sleeping or working, they sat in a trance of concentration while stories were murmered in low, slow voices. Once I reached out and touched Salvatore; he was quite warm, almost as though feverish. I tried to break Augustine's concentration to get some attention from her. But I saw that the moment she turned to respond to me she lost her heat and began to shiver as I did.

Finally, I rolled myself up in my blanket, burrowed deep into the dry leaves and hugged my little goat closely, dozing as the children did, trying not to wake and wonder if I could survive the winter.

Just at the point where I had numbed myself to this state of hibernation, the whole village roused itself. Everyone in the ka got up and began to clean it out. I protested the loss of heat, but the activity continued and became excited. Everyone washed and wrapped himself in blankets and mats. We were going out.

"It is the ceremony of light," said Chil-sing, with a happy smile.

The sky was gray, the paths muddy, but the wind was still for once. We followed the circular paths, dancing and jumping and singing to keep warm—or rather, they danced and sang—I shivered and stumbled along behind them.

Everyone hurried inward on the paths toward the Life Tree, which glowed skeletal and red. Someone had lit a fire near it. Children danced around the fire. They lit long stems of dry grass and were lifted up to tie the glowing bits to the wet, bare branches of the tree, where they blazed, sputtered and quickly died.

Everyone circled the Life Tree and sang a song which I will roughly paraphrase:

> Already far from Home
> Far from the source of life
> We have strayed further
> To the deepest dark.
>
> Now turn, turn turn
> We now turn back
> Turn, turn,turn
> Back to the light of life.
>
> Rejoice in darkest night
> Dark night brings deep dreams
> The farther we go
> The closer to our Home.
>
> So turn, turn, turn
> We now turn back
> Turn, turn, turn
> Back to the light of life.

We continued to circle the fire and the tree until the fire

burned out, exhausting the last bit of stored fuel. Then we filed into the la-ka, where the remaining provisions were parceled out, and we carried them, still singing, back to the ka. I had to admit I felt quite cheered up by then.

That night the stories continued long after dark, everyone taking a turn at them. When my turn came I told the Christmas story, which was accepted as happily as any of the others (several of which it resembled), especially any details about the animals in the stable who gathered around the new born baby.

"And which was the child's animal?" asked Jamal.

"A lamb," I answered, and Sbgai grinned as he patted the neck of his lamb.

But the damp cold hung on in the following weeks. When our provisions ran out I went out to the fields to dig up root vegetables. By now all the others were nearly always in the trance or doze that would keep them alive. I again began to wonder if I would make it.

Several things convinced me that I would not. The cold, the hunger, yes. And not only those, but what they brought.

Augustine was far from me now, maintaining her dream-state. Perhaps, I thought, it was she and the brief daily sessions in the hol-kas that had kept my monsters at bay. Now they were on me in full force. We were all hallucinating, people moving in and out of dreams they told as they lived them. But all my shadows were back. In my weakened state, I knew that I could not keep up the battle against them.

I not only dreamed them, I saw and felt them, oozing out of the mats of the ka, howling with the wind. I struggled and screamed, but when I saw through them to the people lying or sitting around me, no one had moved. I lived in my nightmare; awake or asleep there was no escape.

I staggered out to the fields, afraid to look back to see what pursued me. I hunted for roots, though we had already dug up the crop. I felt that if I could keep moving I might keep the shadows at a distance. But I took them everywhere with me. I went out every day for seven days, then collapsed and waited to die.

I didn't, of course. I simply writhed and sweated and screamed. And I could see that no one heard. Our bodies lay together, our feet pointing to the center of our sleeping wheel, while I and my terrors floated above, and I knew that, weightless as I now was, the shadows would absorb me, and I would die. I wanted to cry out for Augustine but was afraid that waking her would endanger her life.

Sure that this was finally the end, and without the strength or will to fight, I let go. I let go of something indefinable—my life, I suppose.

Then I opened my eyes to look at the shadow which moved in closest to me.

It was me, of course. They were all me, in one rotten form after another. There were twelve of me and we did the dance of the numbers, in the empty la-ka which echoed with our yells and screams and stomps. For an eternity we did the dance of the numbers. But in the pit was a great roaring fire. And every one of me fought not to be thrown into the fire, and screamed in pain of consumption by the fire. The pain was real, the deaths were real.

There is no point in my trying to describe each loathsome identity of me, each frantic gesture, each screeching immolation. I could see my body in the sleeping wheel below. I watched it crawl to the edge of the ka and lick water from the mud outside. And I went on with the dance.

After eons there were two of me left, facing each other across the fire pit. One of me was a woman, a hundred women, all the women, hurt, enraged and furious, that I had ever known. One of me was a man, myself, every rotten, opportunistic, cruel, avaricious and vain self I had ever been.

We faced each other and danced obscenely, cruelly, furiously, ever alert, watching. For every move of the dance was a threat, an aggression demanding simultaneous reaction and defense.

It seemed to go on for years. I was tired. I had to destroy her. I tried every way I could think of, but she anticipated my every move. Then she grabbed the initiative and I was defensive until I could get it back. But I was so tired. Finally I stopped doing anything but defensive, complementary moves. I let her dictate the dance.

Her movements slowed, and she became dim. She darkened as if turning into a shadow again. And her movements were less threatening, finally not threatening at all, but neutral. I continued to follow her. And her movements became great sweeps of grace, of joy, that I followed in perfect simultaneity as she turned darker, darker, black.

"Augustine!" I cried and threw myself forward.

Clasped tightly in each other's arms, we fell into the fire.

I opened my eyes. Faint sunlight peeked through a rip in the mat above me.

"Augustine." She was standing before me, her belly huge. She was smiling.

"Come and see," she said. I followed her out of the ka. The earth was still wet and chill. But the air was different.

Augustine led me to the wall. "See," she said, and bent down to point. Growing out of the rock from a crevice too thin to contain more than a few grains of dirt, was a bright red flower. "And look there."

We held hands and pointed to the flowers. Other kin came out and did the same. A few attempted a hop or a skip, but reeled weakly against one another, laughing. Then some walked inward toward the la-ka while others cut over the walls and went outward.

"Where are they going?"

"Some to the la-ka to build a fire. It will not be easy. They will tear down dried roof mats for the fire. Some will gather new grass from the fields and others, the blossoms and herbs from the walls. And others will bring pots of water. In a little while we will have hot herb broth and we will drink to the new life."

"I should help."

"Not today," she said. "Rest with me and hold my hand. It is not every winter that a man dances the numbers dance to its finish and comes out of the pit as one."

I stared at her. "Did I talk, scream?"

"Not your body, not a sound."

"Then how did you know?"

Her blue eyes stood out large in her thin face. "Was I not there with you? Did I not jump into the fire with you when you called? I will always, always be with you when you call."

Four

We sat on the stone wall in the pale sunlight, holding hands. It must seem strange that I did not immediately begin to question Augustine on how it was that she had contrived to enter my dream, or how common a practice this was or how many other such feats she might be able to perform. I had heard of ESP and Indian rope tricks. I was neither willing nor unwilling to believe that some people could do such things. I had always been indifferent, since it seemed not worth the effort to separate the genuine from the false. Most of all, I had been put off by the sort of people who were interested in such things. They were always weird in one unattractive way or another, and their interest in the occult had a musty, sexual odor—old ladies with crimped hair and painted faces who hadn't been laid in twenty years.

A rational man is not equipped to ask the right questions about a non-rational event. I felt as I had on my first climb up the hill, when I saw the expanse of ocean around me. What I confronted was not simply the physical fact of the ocean, but the possibilities arising from that fact.

Similarly, I now knew that I was not among a primitive people practicing mumbo-jumbo that occasionally resulted in an interesting effect. There had been no tricks, no voodoo charms, no magic words—but when I needed her, Augustine had been able to . . .

" . . . to save me," I said aloud.

She smiled and shook her head. "No one can save another."

"To help, then."

"All right, to help."

"But I don't feel any different," I said.

She laughed. "We never do, not for long. That is why we must keep dreaming."

The last of the people had passed by us going toward the la-ka. We fell in behind them. Everyone looked thin, but amazingly fit. I saw no one staggering. No one looked ill. No one short-cut over the walls, but all walked steadily and slowly toward the la-ka.

It was another sign of the magnificent health of the people. I rarely saw anyone ill. The people believed that ill health began with donagdeo—acts which would disturb or decrease their ability to dream, and resulted from accompanying states of imbalance. That was why they immediately went to a hol-ka, at the first sign of such imbalance. A session in the hol-ka generally averted illness. In case of accident, a person spent a day or two in the hol-ka, then went back, as much as possible while healing, to his usual activities. Actually the people did not believe in accidental injuries; and a person's illnesses were his own responsibility. I don't mean to imply some magic immunity from biological fate, only that illness was over with quickly, either through recovery or death. There was no chronic dis-ease.

We stopped at the pool, which was full of fresh water running over the stones which lined it, and scooped water up to our faces. We sprinkled water over the roots of the tree, still bare and black, twining hundreds of branches from the three main branches growing out of the great trunk.

Inside the la-ka the atmosphere was unusually quiet. A great fire blazed in the pit, surrounded by pots, and all the people sat looking at the flames. They seemed to be in a trance as deep as the one through which many had survived the winter. We sat between Chil-sing and Salvatore, whose eyes remained fixed on the flames. Augustine immediately dropped my hand and began to look at the flames. I could tell that she had instantly put herself into a trance. I sat looking at the flames too, my mind racing. After my latest experience I had no doubt that something extraordinary would happen.

Someone who must have been the oldest person on the island got up from a step near the fire. He or she, skeletal and hairless, was helped by two children who could not have been more than three years old. They stood on either side of her as she went down on her knees, keeping each hand on one little shoulder for support. The little ones, muffled up in their blankets, stood very straight and solemn, as though conscious of great responsibility. Then the old one spoke.

"Has any kin been chosen?"

There was silence as the old eyes peered around the la-ka. The people seemed to be holding their breath.

Then Salvatore turned to me and said, "Now."

"What?"

"If you want to go back," he said, "you must stand up now."

"Back? Back to the world. You mean right now?"

"This is the time. Before we break the fast."

"Has any kin been chosen?" repeated the old one.

I turned to look at Augustine, but her eyes were on the fire. I turned back to Salvatore. "Can't it wait till tomorrow, or a few days, when I feel stronger?"

He was shaking his head even before I finished the sentence. "This is the only time we are able. If you do not go now you will have to wait until after the next winter fast."

I believed him. I was past questioning or calling the people primitive or superstitious. I believed that if I wanted to leave I would have to say so, now. "Has any kin been chosen?"

I sat with every muscle tensed, ready to rise and tell them I wanted to go. But I did not move. The silence held for another minute. Then a great sigh filled the la-ka, as though all had let go their breath with relief. And the people jumped up and began to embrace one another, to greet the ones they had not seen since the ceremony of light. While the pots warmed, the people talked and laughed, broke out in little songs here and there, and took turns standing near the fire.

"What made you decide to stay?" asked Augustine.

"I don't know. Maybe it was you." I had meant to please her, but she only frowned.

"I hope not. One person is not enough."

"Perhaps I want to see the child when it comes."

"Perhaps."

"I didn't really decide to stay. I meant to stand up and say I wanted to go. But . . . I didn't . . . couldn't move."

She looked relieved. "That is a real decision."

"Are you glad I'm staying?"

"Yes, of course." It was almost casual. She was still a mystery to me. At one moment she could say she would be with me whenever I called, and at another, she seemed almost indifferent to me.

As I looked at her a tiny, almost transparent butterfly flittered down through the air and landed on her shoulder.

"Your friend's back," I said.

She laughed and walked away to embrace one of the children. I turned to Salvatore and Sbgai. "So it looks like I'll stay another year."

"Good, my kin," said Sbgai, throwing his hairy arms around me.

"Could you really have sent me back?"

"I think so," said Salvatore.

"How?"

He sighed. "It cannot be explained. Many things are needed. The person must be called, chosen."

"How?"

"In his dreams. In the winter fast. Something happens, I do not know what, because I have never been called. Then when we come together after the fast, when we are most purely in our dreams, we can send the chosen kin out to the rest of the world."

"Does someone go every spring?"

"Not every spring." He smiled. "No, as you see, no one was called this spring."

"You seem glad of that."

"Of course. No one wants to go."

"Then why would anyone go?"

"If he was chosen, he must. And, you see, it is always a strong dreamer, a great dreamer, who is chosen. The loss to us is terrible. That is why we are glad when no one is chosen."

"What would happen if someone were chosen and didn't go?"

"Then Ata would be no more."

"What do you mean?"

"The world would be destroyed."

"By whom?"

Salvatore spread his arms out as if to include the whole universe.

"Are you telling me that every spring, well, not every spring, but sometimes in spring, you must sacrifice one of your best to insure survival of Ata?"

"That is true. It is a sacrifice."

I smiled. "Hey, you weren't going to kill me, were you?"

"No, why would we do such a thing? We were going to try to send you back."

I believed him. "But what you say resembled old religious rites. The spring sacrifice. We don't actually kill anyone anymore, but people used to. Some still kill animals that way."

"Yes, I know. It is a misunderstanding, a false imitation. Unfortunate. How can death be a sacrifice? Death is only release into dreams; it can only be bad if one's dreams are bad. But to be sent into the world you left . . . can you imagine what that is like for a person used to the ways of

Ata, used to living for his dreams? A world where all is donagdeo, where the most admired are the farthest from their dreams. Where empty speech is praised. Where noise is constant. Where people learn hate and suspicion of all, even of those they sleep with. Where people must feed themselves, or have the food snatched away from them. Where instead of the sacred dreams of the la-ka people fill themselves with diversions that are like pain-killers, only adding addiction to dis-ease. Where all the people are like starving beasts, catching a glimpse from time to time of the great feast that lies before them, but kept from it by an invisible wall of fear and pride and superstition, crying, clawing at one another, despairing, and, by their acts, creating nightmares so that they learn to despise and fear that which would save them . . ."

"Then why send someone back?"

"All that I have described. Is it true of the world you left?"

"Yes, it is true."

"And have you ever asked yourself, how is it that this world has not yet destroyed itself?"

"Yes, everyone asks that, especially these days."

"It would have destroyed itself. The complete discon-nection from the dream, total donagdeo, is destruction. When that possibility is imminent, someone is called, some kin of Ata, someone very strong. This kin is sent back, is sacrificed, is sent to live among those on the edge of destruction. The human race is like a suicide, perched on the edge of a cliff, wavering, teetering. When she is about to fall over the edge, one of us goes out and, using all the strength he has, makes a wind that blows against the falling, keeps humanity wavering on the brink. Do you

139

understand what I am telling you?"

"I don't know. But anyway, why? Why not let her jump? Why bother?"

"What, and go back to start all over, from the very beginning." Salvatore shook his head and put his hand on my shoulder. "You still do not understand. You will, you will understand more, by and by. Why not let her jump? But my dear kin, did you suppose that we of Ata are not a part of the human race and all a part of us? We are all kin, and though we have lost them, we must draw them all back again if any of us is to go to . . . to what we are for. One cannot go alone; it must be all or none, you see. A hard law, but inexorable."

"I thought there were no laws on Ata."

"That is a law. Like gravity."

"How do you know so much about the world?"

"I know. I have seen it."

"In your dreams?"

"Yes, enough of it."

"You are of that world."

"Yes, we are all kin."

"No, I mean you came from there. I've finally figured out some of the history of Ata. Long ago, how long ago I'm not sure, some of you started leaving that world, maybe when industrialization began. You found this island, uncharted, deserted, and settled on it. Since then, people have come here, usually by accident. You set up a different way of life here, and you've stumbled onto—
—excuse me— you learned how to use some psychological forces that I don't understand yet. And to keep from being over-run you've had to . . . "

But Salvatore had been steadily shaking his head and

smiling as I spoke. "You have reversed it. But look, the broth is ready now. Let us drink. Then, within three days, you will hear the whole story from the beginning. It is part of the spring ceremonies."

"The history of Ata?" I asked.

"The history of the world," he replied.

People were walking down the steps, picking up a shell from the pile near the fire, uncovering the clay pots, and dipping the shell into them. First the old were fed, and then came the children. Then the pregnant women; there were four of them, including Augustine, all of them, it seemed, close to giving birth. The other three were, however, very young. After Augustine had been fed, she dipped a shell into the pot and came toward me. I sipped the tepid broth. It tasted like strong aromatic tea.

"I tasted this before," I said.

"Yes, in the hol-ka, when you were sick and hurt. It is made from herbs."

The broth was warming and stimulating. I felt much stronger after taking it. When we emptied the pots, they were filled again and placed near the fire. People continued to feed the fire with mats torn from the roof. We stayed in the la-ka for two days and two nights, dozing, sipping the strengthening broth, enjoying the warmth of the fire.

On the third day we arose at dawn. "Bath day," said Augustine.

As we left the la-ka, I saw that the old Life Tree had burst into bloom. The light breeze had already blown some of the white blossoms to the ground. We picked up the scattered petals as we passed under the tree. We filed down to the beach and scattered the petals over the water.

Then everyone threw his tunic ahead of him as we entered the cold water. It was still almost icy, and our bath was not much more than a hasty ritual. But I did feel refreshed and clean as I came out, and we all put on new tunics before we filed back to the la-ka.

More broth, a few roots and some tender leaves made our feast, and then we settled down for the telling of the history which Salvatore had promised me.

It was told, acted, danced and sung; the complete enactment took seven days and could have filled many books. What I produce here is a faulty division of it (since there were overlapping parallel strains of the story) and not really a summary, but rather an introduction or heading for the subject of each day's ritual.

The First Day–Creation

This day was given entirely to tellings and enactments of the creation of man, substantially the creation story I have written earlier, but with important additions. According to this history man was created on Ata as the climax in a long series of creations, and his destiny was to participate in further creations. "That was why he was born a dreamer," went one of the songs.

The Second Day–Exile

This day was given over to the recitation of a long series of mass exiles from Ata. It seems that almost immediately man misunderstood his role, or was not himself a sufficiently advanced creation to quite understand his role. He began his work of creation, but impatiently, not dreaming his creation first, creating things that were merely things, empty of the dream. Then he became absorbed in the things, fell further and further from the dream and from his true destiny. For many ages these rebel-thing-makers rose to domination over dreamers, enslaving and decimating the population of Ata, then making boats in which they left the island. The few survivors began again, only to be again oppressed and destroyed by a new restless, impatient generation, who, when they had done the limit of damage, again left. Somehow there were always a few left to start again.

These defeats came to an end gradually as the exiles spread over the earth. In their dreams, the ones left on Ata could see how the exiles lived in restless misery throughout the world. Desire to leave Ata lessened; the people kept to their obedience to the dream, no longer tempted to seek short cuts.

The Third Day—Return

This day was given mostly to a description of the exiles spread over the earth, denying or forgetting that Ata existed, except in the continual hints of their own dreams. (Atans knew that their dream stories existed in countless versions throughout the world, despised or tolerated or, even worse, twisted into dogmatic law.) The dreams persisted, and so did the urge to return to Ata.

There were many stories of people setting out in ships to find—what? They did not know. But almost from the beginning of the exiles, there were attempts to return, people continually setting off for some place they could not name, but always a place full of rich treasure, where life was happy.

Such explorations, of course, failed.

But once a ship actually did succeed in reaching Ata. The long lost kin were greeted with joy by the Atans, who believed their long wait was over and that all their kin would now begin to return to obedience to their dream.

But they were disastrously mistaken. The people from the ship had been gone too long. Through many generations they had suffered, and the more they sought to escape suffering, the more suffering they created. They sought treasure, but did not recognize the treasure Ata offered. When they landed on the shores of Ata they brought back greed and cruelty against which the Atans had no weapons. Within a few months they had practically wiped out the population. They loaded the rest, along with their animals, in their ship, to take back with them as slaves. They themselves stayed in the la-ka.

But once more the kin of Ata were saved. During the night before they were to sail, a great tidal wave hit the island. The ship survived, but the island was flooded and all in the la-ka drowned. The next day the remaining kin of Ata came out of the ship and reclaimed their island, to begin again.

After this narrow escape a great dream shared by all survivors promised them that in the future no invaders would find Ata and that only individuals, by desire and faith in their dreams, could return.

The Fourth Day—Building

This day the stories covered ages through which the present way of life of Ata was designed by the dreams, in every way from the plan of the village to the use of the hol-kas. It was paralleled by building of exile kingdoms throughout the earth, continual explorations and searches, continual warring among exiled kin, so that the more perfect in dreaming Atans became the greater the multiplication of donagdeo throughout the rest of the earth became. This part of the history was repetitious and depressing.

The Fifth Day–The Sacrificial Exiles

It was unclear exactly when the sacrificial exiles began. Sometimes there was one every spring; sometimes many years passed before a strong dreamer was sent back to live briefly among the millions lost to Ata. This day was given to the stories of the many who went, and what they did. It was the closest thing I ever saw to hero worship among Atans. And, of course, a few of the heroes and heroines were startingly familiar to me.

The Sixth Day–The True Return

These stories were more optimistic than those of the past two days. Some kin in the world, the history ran, had actually perceived the truth of their dreams, somehow overcame the beliefs under which they grew, and tried to live according to the dream. Some did so in a partial way, some learned the way and then lost it, some lived entirely by Atan ways—but not for long, for the world generally destroyed them. But every one of them, however briefly he or she touched the dream, was a cause for celebration, and while the sacrificial exiles from Ata were never mentioned by name, on this day the songs of celebration were made up of lists of names of those in the outside world who had made the return.

The physical return, a rare occurrence, was seen as a precious gift and an omen of great importance which was not yet understood. I understood now why I had been welcomed so reverently, if mistakenly.

The Seventh Day—Rededication

This day was mainly one of ritual rededication to the purpose of Ata: to survive, to persist in the dream until the lost Atans returned, not in ships or planes, but one by one through their dreams; to hold on until man could begin again to fulfill his destiny.

The next morning all went back to the regular routine. I got up and faced Salvatore as he recited his dream, but when he had finished, I realized that I had nothing to say.

"I did not dream," I said. "Or if I did, I don't remember."

Salvatore nodded. He did not seem to see anything strange in this. But I was a bit disappointed. I thought that, now that my monsters had at last been laid to rest, I might dream something more interesting.

As we went into the fields I noticed that Augustine stopped at a hol-ka. I made no comment, but kept an eye on it throughout the morning. She did not come out. When the sun was overhead, I went to sit outside her hol-ka, trying to decide whether I should disturb her. Just when I was ready to crawl in, worrying that she may have gotten sick or fainted, she emerged, head first, moving on her back instead of crawling on her immense belly.

"Are you all right?"

"Yes."

I brought her some water, then called my little goat, who had just dropped her kid. I made Augustine lie under the goat and squirted some milk into her mouth. In a moment she sat up, thanked me, and then stood.

"You're not going to work."

"Just for a little while. Then I will return to the hol-ka."

"Why do you spend so much time there?"

"My time is near." She did not want to talk. She spent most of the day, and those following, in the hol-ka. I came to her several times a day, bringing water and milk and fresh greens.

As for me, sex surged up in me after the fast, as if I were sixteen again. Of course, I did not approach Augustine, but I found myself counting off the time—even after the baby was born I would have to leave her alone for a while. The next day as she sipped water from my hand, she smiled at me and said, "Many girls are warm and eager after the fast. They will not refuse you."

"Do you always know what I am thinking?"

"Not always. Often."

"You would not be jealous if I lie with that girl?" I pointed toward a nearby teenager who was scattering seed.

Augustine thought for a moment then shook her head. I could see that she meant it, and I was a little disappointed.

" Would you do it, if I were sick or something?"

"I don't think so."

"Ah, see, you don't approve. Why?"

"For me it would be donagdeo."

"But not for me?"

She was silent for a moment. "That depends on where you are in your dreams. I can't know. Only you can find out. If sex for you is still simple, as it is for the children, for the goat . . . "

"You don't care?"

"What has it to do with me?" she asked. She began to slip back into the hol-ka.

"Wait a minute," I said. "One question. How is it four women are having children at the same time, and only four?"

"Those are two questions."

"All right, two questions."

"The spring is the best time to have a child. And we do not have too many children, not to go too far from the twelve times twelve number of the dream."

"But how do you arrange this?"

"By not making love when we would conceive. Man is always fertile, but women only for a few hours from one full moon to the next. Surely you know that."

"Of course, but it's a pretty hit and miss way to . . . "

"It is not hit and miss."

"You mean you know the exact time when you are fertile?"

"Yes."

"How do you know?"

She shrugged. "How do you know you are thirsty? You know. The young girls do not know so well, so usually they are the ones who have a child, once or twice, as I had a child when I was very young."

"And you would not have had this one if I had not forced you."

She squeezed my hand and smiled tolerantly, as she often did when I fell into meaningless small-talk, then eased herself back into the hol-ka.

A few days later we were all summoned to the la-ka in the middle of the day. One of the girls had announced that morning that her pains had begun. She had stayed in the village, sitting under the Life Tree with three boys until the pains were very close together. Then we were all summoned. Chil-sing explained to me on the way in.

"Giving birth is a very hard thing. We all try to help."

"How can we help?"

"We try to take some of the pain on ourselves, to share it. We try to give some of our strength for the hard work. We try to make the girl feel happy that, once she has done this, she need no longer carry the burden of the child alone. Then she will labor in joy. At the least, we give the warmth of our bodies surrounding her."

When we entered the la-ka, the girl was standing near the fire-pit with three boys. Each person who entered stopped by her to embrace her or to kiss her. She was smiling and seemed quite relaxed, but every two or three minutes her eyes blinked rapidly and she trembled as if gripped and shaken by a great fist. Sometimes she would sit down or lie down. Then she would get up and walk around, leaning on two of the boys.

"Who are those three boys?" I asked.

"They are the fathers," said Chil-sing.

"They can't all be the father," I retorted.

Chil-sing shrugged. "One must be, but how can they know which one? So all must do their part. She lay with all three."

The walking and sitting went on for hours, while everyone sat in silent concentration.

Then, as she stood leaning on a boy, a great gush of water poured from under her tunic. The boys tipped her back, supporting her so that she lay half sitting up. Sounds of gutteral straining came from her throat, no screams, but moans of the agony of an effort which reached the limits of human endurance. Groans were rising all around me, and tears poured down contorted faces.

It lasted for about half an hour, and it seemed like forever. I had never seen a birth. I felt sick and ashamed of my weak stomach, but when we heard the cry of the baby, Salvatore turned to me and said, "Fine, my kin, you did your part well."

"I have never seen this before," I said.

"Why not? Many, many more children are born in the outside world."

"But not where they can be seen."

"That must make it very hard for the mother."

"No, no, it is not . . . "

"How do you know if you have never seen?"

Everyone was taking deep breaths now and leaning back or stretching. The girl who had given birth raised her head and nodded. Then everyone began to get up. They all went straight down to the place where she lay, and everyone helped to clean up the blood and to make a fresh place for her and the baby to lie near the fire pit. She would stay in the la-ka, Salvatore told me, constantly attended by the fathers of the child, near the warm fire, for three days, then would take her baby and walk back to her ka.

As we left Augustine took my hand.

"You should not have been here," I said.

"Why not?"

I could not say anymore. I was terrified for her. She was no longer young, and in these crude conditions, anything could happen. "Your . . . your mother . . . "

" . . . died in childbirth here? Yes, but she had just come from the world and was greatly weakened by it. I will not die."

"How many fathers attended you in your first birth?"

She looked at me. Then I saw her eyebrow rise and her mouth curve into a smile.

"How many?" I demanded.

She laughed outright and pinched me. Her greenish butterfly seemed to dance around her ear. Then she pretended to count on her fingers, exhausting all of them and then starting again.

I laughed. "I'm sorry. Sorry. I should be afraid for your safety and I'm jealous over something that happened years ago."

"I would rather have you suffer jealousy than fear, but rather you not suffer at all, my love."

I was faithful to Augustine during this time. It was the first time I had ever denied myself sex for any reason. I jokingly told myself that it would be a new experience, and that maybe the deprivation would start me dreaming again, if only the sex dreams of an adolescent. I wavered from time to time when I saw the young girls smiling invitingly at every male they saw. But I could not look at one of those children without seeing the straining face of the girl in childbirth. Somewhat surprisingly to me, I found that I did not want to be the cause of that.

And the older women, less likely to become pregnant, stuck to one partner. Now that I knew the people better, I could identify couples, some of whom slept together in the same ka, some of whom did not. I gradually learned that such "marriages" might last one season or many, or even—but rarely—for a lifetime. But there was no promiscuity among the mature, and no parenthood, except for me.

"I seem to have upset the natural order of things," I told Salvatore.

He smiled. "When outsiders come, they often conceive children. That is what varies our physical type. That is healthy. But in general our numbers remain the same and not many children are born. No woman wants to go through pregnancy and birth again once she knows what it is. Too many children are donagdeo."

I nodded. "Starvation."

"Much worse. Children are . . . they are bundles of appetites, hungers. They come straight out of the dream, yet are farthest from it. Their humanity is so raw, so . . . "

I laughed. "Screaming egotists. It's interesting you admit that. We don't, out in the world. We call them innocent, pure . . . "

"They are pure desire. And they must not be thwarted, for if they are they will never grow. They must give up gradually of their own free will. To force is donagdeo." I remembered that my gang had been made up of children. "They must try everything, have everything—too many would destroy our way of life faster than any invasion from outside."

"So that's why you play down sex, dress alike, and cover yourselves."

Salvatore shook his head. "Why would we want to play down the creative force of the universe?"

I tried to explain to him what I meant, making comparisons between Ata and the outside world, but he kept insisting that what I called an emphasis on sex outside was really a total loss and de-emphasis by Atan standards. When he saw that I was talking about the physical act of sex he looked shocked. "But is that all you mean by sex?" And we didn't seem to be able to get beyond that; we got bogged down in translation.

I changed the subject. "But is there never any jealousy, any possessiveness, any . . . "

He laughed. "Oh, yes, we are of the human race, aren't we? Look around you, my kin, and you will see all the emotions and desires of the world being battled. Jealousy is such an ugly feeling. One would do anything rather than be filled with that sick feeling. We struggle against it. Sometimes it can ruin dreams for a whole season. So we do our best to avoid it if we can, to lose it if we have it." He put his hand on my shoulder. "My kin, we are as weak as all people. But when we fall, we get up again to live for the dream."

The other two girls gave birth within a week. During the second birth, Augustine remained in a hol-ka, where she had been for two days. No one said anything when I sat beside her hol-ka waiting. At dusk, Augustine came out. "It is time for me to go to the Life Tree," she said.

I said she should go directly to the la-ka, where a warm fire would be blazing, but she refused. All night she sat under the Life Tree. I stayed with her, and at times I asked if she needed anything or if there was something I could do. Then I saw that I was only interrupting her concentration. She had put herself into a trance, was quite warm, and made no sign of feeling the pains.

Just as the sky was becoming gray, she opened her eyes, got up, and went into the la-ka. Within a few minutes all the people of the village were there, though no one had been sent to get them. I helped her to lower herself to the bed of clean grass that had been made beside the fire, and I held her in my arms as she lay back against me, her knees bent and her feet flat on the ground. She seemed to be looking at the fire from between her knees, over her great belly. I saw the belly suddenly flatten somewhat and heard the rush of water. Then I watched it heave in great, steady, constant contractions, like the heaving of earth in an earthquake. I wished with all my might to take some of the pain from her. I looked at her face, expecting to see it contorted with the effort, but her face was still, serene, gleaming in the glow of the fire on which her narrowed eyes fixed in deep concentration.

I heard the baby cry. Augustine's belly heaved again. Then her eyes blinked; she looked down to the pool between her legs, picked up the baby and lay it across her belly. She winced slightly as the afterbirth was expelled, then looked up at me and smiled. Her eyes closed and she fell into a deep sleep, there in my arms.

I cannot describe the feeling I had during those few minutes when she slept in my arms with the slimy little baby lying across her. Sweat and tears ran down my face as I held her and the people came to clean up, to wash the baby and to prepare a clean place for us to rest beside the fire. The baby was a girl, like Augustine, but the color of brown sugar.

We stayed in the la-ka for three days, and I had Augustine entirely to myself, like a child with a favorite toy. It was like a honeymoon, except that instead of sex play, I fed her and watched her nurse the baby, a voluptuous experience for both of them, after which Augustine lay like a woman satiated with sex. I fed her and petted her and held the baby when she was not nursing. On the third day Augustine bounced up in a very businesslike way, as if we had indulged ourselves long enough, and I followed her back to the ka, carrying the baby.

As we entered it early in the morning, Augustine said to everyone, "Now we are twelve again, a complete sleeping wheel."

I did not get to enjoy my lugubrious paternity for long. Except when Augustine was nursing the baby, she seldom touched it, nor did I. The others took turns caring for the infant, rocking it, holding it, cleaning it. The baby never cried. At her first restless grunts of hunger, someone heard and brought her to Augustine to nurse. At any other stirrings, she was held and rocked. Her first sound was a coo of pleasure at recognizing Chil-sing's face as he bent over her.

After a few weeks, the baby was held and played with by the older children from different kas. She was truly, from the beginning, not our baby. She belonged to everyone.

To my increasing astonishment, I remained celibate until one day Augustine took me by the hand and led me to our place by the river where I gently made love to her.

During the period of her nursing, Augustine did no work in the fields, but tended the herbs inside the village with the old and young, or wove mats. A good deal of the time she simply sat in front of the ka in rapt concentration, with a look on her face that seldom left it even when she did other work. There was always a circle of children and animals around her, drawn to her as were the constant attendant butterflies whose size and colors increased as the days grew warmer.

I helped in the planting, and every afternoon, came to take Augustine to our place by the river. She told me that while she was nursing there was no danger of conceiving; we could make love any time. Our lovemaking was different now, not so passionate as before, but steady as the stream that ran beside us. And it was after lovemaking, after our bodily orgasm, that the best of the lovemaking began. After a nap of a few moments, we both awoke to caresses and kisses, long dreamy silences curled in each other's arms, touching that led to no heat of passion but held us as if floating in a warm ocean. Sometimes we forgot to make love at all and simply lay together suspended.

At these times she was more willing to talk, if I started. This was how I learned about names.

"What shall we name the baby?" I asked her one day.

"We do not name it."

"Who does?"

"The child, kin itself must find a name."

"In a dream?"

"Yes."

"When does this dream come, the dream that gives her a name?"

"It varies. Jamal dreamed his name, but that is rare. My name came only shortly before you came here. Some are very old before they learn their name."

"I am still nameless."

"Yes. Some have many names before they die. A few have died nameless."

"I'll never get a name. I seem to have stopped dreaming since the winter fast."

She didn't answer. I was getting so that I could tell when she drifted away from me. I could call her right back again and usually did, but sometimes I just watched her instead. Gradually I stopped being jealous of her drifting to some place where I could not follow, and simply enjoyed watching her face. For if I let her stay there, instead of calling her back to me, I seemed to get some echo, some reflection of what it was that drew her away. It was like a warm glow coming from her blue eyes.

Except for the hour or two I spent with her every afternoon, my days were filled with activity. My first thought was to try to increase the food supply so that the winter fast need not be so severe. I was told that last winter had been longer than usual, but that all had come through very well. No one tried to stop me from making their agricultural methods more efficient. No one even mentioned the fact that I knew nothing about agriculture.

The planting, like the layout of the village, was done according to dreams. There was what looked like a hodge-podge of growth, nothing planted in rows as I was used to seeing it, an incredible variety of plants all mixed together, planted in rotation at times and in places suggested in dreams. Some plots were individually planted, according to someone's dream of the night before, and

large areas beyond the hills, which I felt should be cultivated, were left alone because they had not yet appeared
in anyone's planting dreams. Sometimes an area was
abandoned for a season or more because it was, in a
dream, shown unfit, and that area became the latrine area
for the time. I suppose we were fertilizing the soil and
helping it to recover for more planting.

The first task of small children was to pick bugs off the
plants or keep away the animals, like my little goat. The
rest of us planted and tended the soil with our hands and
feet and the crudest of sticks or bones. When I described
the farm machinery of the world, the people only smiled.
"You mean you must dig up metal, and prepare it, and
design machinery, and build machinery and . . . " They
made the process sound like enormously more work than
we were doing.

It was only much later that I came to any realization of
the intricate pattern of cultivation. Plants which needed a
great deal of sun formed umbrellas over those that needed
shade. Certain plants attracted bugs antagonistic to those
attracted by the nearest other plants. Seemingly irregular
swirls of planting patterns repeated themselves, year after
year, possibly following lines of underground channels of
water. Crops flourished where dreams directed they be
planted.

The people were right. They operated with knowledge
far deeper than I could ever reach—I who could not even
dream.

There was constant work to do. But if everyone helped
there was never too much to do. There was always time
for the hol-ka or for a long walk around the island to
gather wild grass for the weaving. And the yield was

always enough. During that year, Augustine came out to the fields three times. Each time she pointed out an area that had appeared in her dreams and suggested we plant one or two varieties there. Those crops did especially well.

I need hardly add that I knew better than to suggest that we eat birds or animals, or even fish. They would have reacted the same way as if I had told them we should eat the children. When animals died, their bones and skins were taken (after the birds had picked them clean) and used for many things. But no one would have thought of killing any of them.

Some of the bones we used as tools looked suspiciously like those of a human rib cage. "They are," answered Chil-sing. At the next funeral I learned that bodies were taken to a high cliff over the sea where they were picked clean by large birds within a couple of days. Then the skull was buried and the rest of the bones taken back to the village and thrown into the pile of tools, used until broken and the chips buried in the fields. I might once have been shocked by this. But now it seemed very sensible and in no way disrespectful of the dead. How could there be disrespect toward those who, these people believed, had simply been wholly liberated into their dreams, freed from the bones that now dug the soil?

That funeral was a very interesting one. The boy who died could not have been more than twenty and stood out from the others because he was an exception to their general good health. He was somehow a bit lopsided, incapable of much work, and he hardly spoke at all. He was frail and subject to some kind of seizures that resembled epilepsy. When he came out of a seizure, he could

159

talk without interruption for an hour, listened to intently by the people of his ka, who sometimes told the blazing visions of his seizures to others. He died during one of these seizures.

After the procession to the cliff, where his naked body was laid with arms outstretched and torches burning at the head and the feet, I asked Sbgai about him.

"He was that way from birth," said Sbgai as he lumbered on ahead of me back to the village.

"It was a sickness from birth," I said. "An imperfection."

"Perhaps."

"No, definitely."

Sbgai turned and looked at me. "Perhaps," he declared decisively. Then he went on walking.

"In the world," I said, "he would have been put into a hospital and cared for until he died."

"Hidden from sight," said Sbgai.

"Well, he wasn't a pretty sight," I answered.

"A pretty sight!" Sbgai growled and the dirt seemed to fly from his thumping steps. "A pretty sight! We are here for more than a pretty sight. How do we know the way into the deeper dream? Or the price to pay for it. How can we know anything, we who see so little. Maybe he saw more, maybe less. Who can know?"

"What you're saying is that you can't discriminate between the messages of a prophet and the ravings from a damaged brain."

"Right."

"You know, Sbgai, you are not a primitive people. I think you are a very advanced people. But you have beliefs that I associate with very primitive, unknowing people. Such people often, in their ignorance, consider the crippled or the insane sacred. Such an idea, I'm afraid, could lead to many blind alleys in our search for deeper dreams."

"All are sacred."

"But what if a dream is followed and leads to trouble or hurt?"

"Why, then we see we misunderstood the message of the dream. Common sense! Reason."

"You admit that common sense and reason are useful."

"Indispensible! But they follow the dream."

"In the world, we put them first."

Sbgai laughed and looked at me closely. "And in the world you are able to tell the difference between a prophet and the ravings of a damaged brain?"

When I remained silent he asked me for a definition of "insane." It seemed an ingenuous question, and it was only after I had struggled and sweated and been sent spinning around and around by his demands for clarification that I caught the smile on his face and stopped. He gave a great guffaw and hugged me. It was impossible to be angry. I laughed and said, "Your name is not Sbgai, it's Socrates." I told him a little about Socrates.

"And what happened to him?" asked Sbgai.

"He was executed for corrupting the young."

Sbgai nodded without sadness or regret, but with simple confirmation of the expected. "Probably he was one of us, chosen after the winter fast and sent out." By a quick look at his face I could see that he was not joking.

I gave up trying to be an agricultural expert and simply did my share of the work, following the methods they had arrived at through eons of dreaming. I had no dreams, or none that I could remember.

During the next winter fast I fared better, dozing most of the time like the children. Each time I woke I mended tents or fed people. I brought plenty of water to Augustine, and gave her some of my rations, as she was still nursing. Both she and the baby came through the fast very well. And when we went to the la-ka on the first day of spring, and old Doe, from our ka, asked, "Has any kin been chosen?" it did not even occur to me to stand.

For in the depths of the winter fast I had finally had one fleeting dream, an image which flashed on me and was gone, but which I remembered and resolved to obey. In the image, I saw myself sitting in the center of the la-ka. Behind me, round the fire pit, children were dancing. On every step of the la-ka sat the people of Ata, talking, all talking at once, a great chorus of insistent voices, telling hundreds of dreams. And I sat in the midst of it all, writing.

I began right after the first spring planting. I decided to use a modified Italian alphabet which is almost perfectly phonetic. In this alphabet I could signify nearly all the sounds of the Ata language. I invented five more consonants. There were differences in pitch in pronouncing a word that changed its meaning. These I divided into roughly seven levels which I signified by combinations of dots, dashes and accent marks above the appropriate syllable. I worked all this out by scratching it into the mud surrounding our ka, rubbing it out, changing signs, until finally I felt I had arrived at a written language which, though far from perfect, would serve.

My next problem was to find something more permanent to write on. There was little of any permanence in the village. Tunics and mats were woven and used until they were soiled and ragged, then used as kindling in the fire pit. Aside from the shells and bones (which were buried when they broke) everything was consumed or ploughed under. There was no waste, no pile of debris. I thought, if anything ever happened to Ata, no artifacts would be found, just a spiral stone wall leading to a hole in the ground, and even that hole would probably be filled by the time the archeologists got there.

I considered carving on the stone walls, but that would be tedious work, and slow, with only sharp rocks or bones to use as tools. Finally I decided that hides were the only answer, and asked for some. Chil-sing and Jamal got me some immediately.

After considerable experimentation I managed to make a somewhat rusty looking dye which, with the use of bone splinters, I could scratch into an animal hide.

Every morning I worked in the fields. When the sun was overhead, I lay in the grove by the river with Augustine, who was still nursing the baby, still dreamily confining her activities to the village. Sometimes the baby crawled over us as we lay and talked—or I talked about my plans for writing down all the dreams of Ata. Sometimes the baby napped or played while we made love. Often we were alone, one of the children having adopted the baby, carrying it on his back for a few days, showing up with it only at feeding time.

After my hour with Augustine, my real work, or what I saw as my real work, began. I sat near our ka scratching a story onto the skin while Augustine, like her butterflies, flitted back and forth, tending flowers and herbs. I worked at it until sunset every day, then joined the procession to the la-ka. Now I listened and watched avidly every night.

Half-way through my first attempt I heard, in the la-ka, a somewhat different version of the dream I was writing. "How many versions of that story are there?" I asked Salvatore.

"Many," he answered. "Every dream has many, many versions. Some are very old; then there may be a newer version with a slight change, then a newer one."

"Why don't we just keep the most highly developed?"

"Which one is that?"

"The latest, I mean."

He smiled and shrugged. "It is not so simple. Sometimes an old part of the dream is lost, then picked up again in a new version, fit into the new one, where it says something yet different. To discard anything . . . "

"You mean it's impossible to choose the correct version."

"There is no correct version. All are correct, all are changing." For a few days, I was almost in despair, thinking I had wasted my time in imagining that anything permanent could be made of the complex and shifting mythology of Ata. Even if I managed to get down all versions of one dream, mightn't someone dream a new version the next night, and make my work an incomplete fragment again?

I spent an afternoon in a hol-ka, numb and still, as if I had lost all purpose. But by the time I came out, my mood had changed. What if my task were impossible? Wasn't all art impossible? Art was an attempt to capture the real, to pin it down, to keep it still, so that we can understand. It is impossible. But it is the noblest effort, I told myself. And, until now, I had never tried it. Until now I had merely written.

Suddenly I had something to create, a real art. A real purpose. What if it became a life's work? What if the bare beginnings of the work became a life's work which would have to be carried on by others? Wasn't it enough, wasn't it great to be the beginner of such a work? In all my searches for the orgasmic experience, hadn't I perhaps found it now, in a task that had no end in my lifetime?

I plunged in with redoubled energy. "I am not a dreamer," I told Augustine. "You people are the dreamers. I am to write down your dreams to preserve them. That is why I came here. And that is what I wanted when in my dream I called to you out of the ocean."

I decided that I would start with the great dreams told in the ceremonial meetings of the la-ka. These seemed to be more permanent, dreams that had been dreamed and refined for so long as to reach a permanent state.

It took nearly two months to finish the first skin, the creation dream. First I sketched it out by smearing mud with my fingers on the stone wall. Children and old people gathered round to watch my work. I explained what I was doing and read aloud some of what I had written. The old people offered corrections and suggestions. I listened carefully to them, and began to call them to me to repeat the creation myth over and over again, while I corrected wordings or changed emphasis.

By this time all my notions of the poverty of the Ata language were gone. What I had first learned was the stripped down language of everyday life. The rest of the language, the words they saved for their dreams, was rich and varied, and I learned more and more of it as I sought the right word for each part of the myth.

After six weeks of revision, I simply refused to consider further alterations, and read aloud to Augustine what I now had. She made no criticisms. In two weeks, I had finished the skin, crude and splotchy, but readable.

The reaction of the people was polite interest, almost the same interest they had shown in the ravings of the epileptic as he came out of his seizures. They were neither for nor against what I did. It was what my only dream of the past year had told me to do; so I must do it. I was a little disappointed at first, expecting praise, I suppose, still full of the pride of the intellectual in his feats of abstraction. When I explained how the marks I made were signs for words which told the dream, they nodded. I tried to teach them to read, but no one was interested, not even the children. I began to think the children were reluctant to oblige me because the last time they had followed me, my ideas had led to disaster.

"No, it is not that," said Chil-sing.

"But if you do not learn to read and write, who will carry on my work?" I asked rather fretfully.

"If someone is to do it, his dream will tell him, as yours did. You will live a long time yet. Perhaps the one who will carry on your work is not yet born." That answer satisfied me.

But then I was completely thrown off again. Just after I finished the first skin and had read it to many kin, we went to the la-ka for the evening story, which started, "In the beginning . . . ." I leaned back to relax, thinking this would be the story I had just written down, perhaps with some variations which I would be on the alert for, since I had, by now, memorized it.

But it was not, It was an entirely different story of the creation of Ata. My body snapped forward to listen hard. Old Doe chanted the story in a cracking voice. "And the great dream gathered all its forces together, and the forces twisted and collided and passed through one another and strained until all the forces merged for one instant into the word "space" and there was space. And the space stretched and bent and turned in upon itself until it split into earth and sky. And earth . . . ."

The chant had nearly fifty verses describing an evolutionary chain of one thing growing out of another. At first I thought this was a recent dream of Doe, but gradually I saw people begin to join in the last line of each verse, and children began to act out the "creations" in dance-like mimicry. The whole thing was obviously familiar, and was done in a happy, bouncy style reminiscent of knee-bone-connected-to-the-leg-bone songs.

On the way back to the ka I tried to question Doe about it, but she was too tired to talk. Doe was now one of the oldest kin on the island. I thought of Doe as an old granny; this was how I felt toward all the old, since they, with advanced age, softened into what I saw as a feminine look. As I dropped off to sleep I thought that Doe must be a very important resource for my work, and one not likely to survive long.

The next day, while Augustine and I lay near the river, I asked her about the story of the night before.

"Yes, it is the creation," Augustine replied.

"But there is a different creation story. Which one is correct?"

"Both."

"No, they are not different versions of the same story. They contradict each other."

"Yet they are both true."

I sat in silent exasperation for a few minutes. "How many creation stories are there?"

"Many. I am not sure."

"And they are all true."

"Yes."

"Even if they contradict one another."

"Yes."

"Because somebody dreamed them."

"Yes."

"Augustine, if one of them is true, then another cannot be."

"They are all true. And they are all untrue, as words are always untrue. Words are not dreams. Dreams are not reality. They are only dreams."

"Then what is the reality?"

She smiled at me as if speaking to a child. "How can we know? We can only dream. In the dream, reality comes clothed in coverings we can recognize and describe. We are like children, trying to see the stories in the scratchings you make on the skins. We keep and describe what each of us sees on the skin, but we cannot read the true meanings of the marking there."

"Then you should learn to read and . . . "

"I only use that as a story to explain, but I see I am not clear. When we learn to 'read' the dreams, then . . . then we will perceive and live and be the reality."

"And when will that happen?"

"When all kin live for dreams and obey them."

"All? Everyone in the world? That will never happen."

"It must."

I decided not to get into that argument again. "So you don't literally believe any of the dreams."

"Yes, yes, we believe them all, we keep them all . . ." She saw my confusion. "I can only explain by telling you another story. Let us say that I look at what you write on the skin. I know that the markings mean something that I cannot read. I try to learn to copy them, to preserve them, so that some day I may read them. Since I cannot see the true meaning of each mark you make, I describe the marks in ways I can understand. One mark looks to me like a bird in flight, another like a man bending over, but perhaps the man bending over looks to someone else like a bridge and the bird in flight, like waves of water. We are both right because that is what we see that helps us to remember the mark. And we are both wrong because the marks are not birds or men or bridges, but something else that we do not know how to read."

"Yet, you are obedient to what you do not understand."

"Yes, we must be."

"I don't see how we can live this way."

"But is there another way to live?" Then she laughed, kissed me, and aroused me to love again.

As always, at least temporarily, our lovemaking resolved everything. In the long half-doze afterward when we lay in each other's arms, I told her what I thought I would never say to any woman. "As long as we have this, everything is all right." She did not answer, and I could see that she had drifted away again. "Where are you?" I said, and she immediately focused her eyes on me and smiled. "Right here, whenever you want me."

After a while, the thoughts of my task crept in again, and I began to wonder whether it was worth the trouble, the increasing complications, especially considering the lack of interest of everyone.

"But it is what your dream tells you to do," Augustine answered my thoughts.

"Will I ever learn to read your mind as you do mine?" I asked her.

"That is nothing," she said. "Everyone can do that."

"I can't."

"Let yourself."

"Everything is hard for me. I don't even dream."

"Perhaps you will not dream until you have finished what the last dream told you."

"But that's a life's work!"

"Perhaps. You must let yourself."

My pride balked. "I can't practice this blind obedience as you do, this mindless . . . "

She kissed my cheek and held me as she would if I were crying in pain. "My poor dear, my darling, my love . . . "

When we went back to the village, I went to Doe, who, half-blind, was sitting and weaving a mat without seeing it, so used was she to the feel of the pattern of fibers. I asked her to repeat to me all the creation stories she had ever heard. I had decided that I would devote the rest of the year to collecting and writing down creation stories.

It took all of that. Doe, and some of the other old ones, were cooperative. In the long afternoons I sat outside our ka, listening to the endless creation of the universe. After weeks of listening, I saw a pattern and realized that instead of hundreds of stories I had many versions of twelve basic stories, including the one I had already written down. Now that I could see a clear direction, I felt sure I could condense the rest to eleven basic stories and complete the skins before the next winter fast.

I finished the last one on the day of a terrible rainstorm. And when it came time for the ceremony of lights, the children hung the skins on the Life Tree where they waved in the glow of the fire and the torches. It pleased me to see everyone dance around them, even though they couldn't understand what was written on them. I carried Doe in my arms and wrapped her in the skins before I carried her back to our ka.

Doe never woke from her trance during the fast, and after the drinking of the herb broth on the first spring day, I carried her one last time, in the procession to the cliff. Naked, she was a man, with little flesh left for the birds to pick.

I was eager to begin my work again, deciding to devote myself this year to the history of Ata as told in the spring ceremonies. I had noticed some differences this year from the previous one, but there was still the main, rough chronology of ages which I have already described. I could, I decided, write a brief statement regarding each age on one of seven skins. There would be plenty of room on each skin for adding variations or details later as they appeared. I was more relaxed now about such additions and changes.

Our daughter was weaned now, running about the village like an amber elf. Augustine took up work in the fields again, and we worked silently side by side in the morning. At noon we lay in our grove near the river. The only change was that now Augustine refused me from time to time, when she was menstruating or when she felt fertile. In some ways, these times were better than our lovemaking days. We lay together in a deep rest that seemed no different from the rest that came after orgasm, and I began to notice that on those days I accomplished a great deal of writing in the afternoon.

Once I decided to try continence, but at the end of nine days I was irritable and unable to write. I made love to Augustine clumsily and quickly, like a boy, and then took deep breaths of relief. "So much for channeling sex into creative acts," I said. She didn't answer.

"I can't give it up," I said.

"Of course not. Not unless it gives you up."

"But you could." She didn't answer. "Am I . . . are my demands, my needs, holding you back from . . . "

She shook her head. "You could not hold me back."

"But if you . . . "

She hushed me, making the shrugging motion she often made when she did not want to fall into idle talk.

Soon after that, she stopped refusing me at any time. "Am I guessing at your fertile times now?" I asked, feeling happy that we were becoming that close.

But she shook her head. "No need to worry about fertile times now."

"Menopause? No, you're still having periods."

"But I will not conceive."

She dismissed my questions, but I came to realize that she had attained some further, more advanced control over her body and asked her.

"It is nothing," she said. "Like holding your breath for a few seconds. Now I need never refuse you."

In the afternoons while I wrote, Augustine usually went back to the fields again. I cautioned her against too much heavy work, but then I felt foolish: she would work no more and no less than her dreams told her to. And nothing she did seemed to be work. Everything was a dance. Whether she walked or wove, fed people from the pots or dug in the ground, all her movements were such acts of grace that I often stopped whatever I was doing just to watch her. I was not the only one. There were always people around her, as if she gave out a glow in which kin would warm themselves.

As the days went on, I began to understand why the daily language of Ata lacked tense. There were times for doing certain things: times for planting, for dreaming, for eating, for telling dreams. There were times, but no time.

"Time doesn't exist here," I told Augustine.

"There is only now," she agreed.

"It's because nothing changes."

"Change comes, but very slow and very sudden," she said.

"You contradict yourself."

"Yes," she said.

During the harvest time of that year we celebrated a wedding, the first of few that I saw on Ata. I have said before that marriage as we know it did not exist. The children were usually born to the very young, out of promiscuous relations, in which few fathers could be surely identified. The adults were serially (and often bisexually) monogomous, and the very old, sexless, belonging to the whole population, like children again.

Occasionally, however, a couple stayed together year after year, without pledges or promises, without compulsion. A relation of this sort was neither required nor even hoped for, but a couple who remained together for many, many years was felt to be a great asset to everyone. As it was explained to me, such a couple was thought to have combined into something greater than the sum of their two parts. They often (but not exclusively) dreamed together, and their dreams were considered to be very strong. In general such a couple came very gradually to be viewed with the delight that most societies reserve for small babies—as a precious gift. And sometimes a ceremony honoring their relationship was held: a wedding.

Salvatore and Aya had been together, I was told, since adolescence, when they had two children. In their fifties they were still active sexually. In fact, during the long winter fast they woke together from time to time to make love unashamedly in the warmth of our ka, something I could never quite let myself do, though sometimes in the winter I wanted Augustine. They worked together at most things, yet never seemed to exclude anyone else because of the closeness of their relationship. Sbgai put it very well when he said, "Having four arms instead of two, they can include more people in their embrace."

The wedding was exactly what I might have expected. They started in separate hol-kas where each spent the night. At dawn they came out, were covered with flowers by a group of children, then started to walk the spiral path, hand in hand, inward. As they passed each ka, the people came out, then fell in behind them and followed them to the Life Tree where a brief dance was done. Then all went into the la-ka where the couple stood together near the fire pit while the entire population sang the marriage song.

At the end of the singing, there was more dancing and celebrating, until dark. Then one by one, the people embraced the couple and went out until they were left alone to spend the night in the la-ka, a privilege never taken except by those who had just given birth.

I was greatly moved by the ceremony, and as we walked back to our ka I held Augustine's hand and said, "Perhaps one day you and I will have such a wedding." She did not answer me, and I felt that I had been clumsy. "I don't mean to imply that I could earn such an honor. Look, I'm just trying to tell you I love you; I know I'll always love you. I'm stupid and clumsy about the way I do it, but that's because I'm new at it—at loving. And I like saying it, however awkwardly. I like loving you. I can't imagine living without you."

To my surprise there were tears in her eyes as she turned to look into my face.

"What is it? What did I say wrong?"

"Nothing. Nothing. Only do not hope for a wedding."

"Of course, if you don't want . . . "

But at that, the tears streamed so steadily down her face that I did not want to upset her by saying anymore.

There were several christenings too that fall. This was a ritual performed when a person had dreamed his name.

He told the dream in the la-ka that night, then was formally introduced to all the people. As he walked among them, they each pronounced his name and touched his forehead.

I was amused when the girl in our ka went through the naming ceremony and was christened Herbert.

"But where do the names come from? I mean, I know they come out of dreams, but . . . Herbert?"

Sbgai smiled. "Or a name like mine," he said, "a name like a sneeze."

"I think," said Chil-sing, "that we hear the name of someone out there," he pointed to the ocean, "someone who wants to reach us, someone who feels close."

"It is not that simple," said Salvatore. "There are many reasons for names." That was the closest thing to an argument I ever saw between adults on Ata. And it was ended when both Sbgai and Chil-sing quickly nodded.

By the time winter came I had finished the main outlines of the history of Ata (essentially the story I recorded earlier). I left space on all the skins to add details, variations, even contradictions. Each year I intended to add refinements I would pick up during the spring ceremonies.

During the winter I emerged from sleep every few days to do necessary repairs or get food, but otherwise I was as good a hibernator as any of the children. Whenever I awoke, I saw Augustine in her trance, sitting up, quite warm, with a slight smile on her face. I liked to look at her as I dozed off again.

When spring came I began to see that my original idea of the work must be expanded. And it must have order. There was no sense in simply setting down any tale that was brought to me. I had to find categories for them.

I made rough divisions of dream stories. At the top were the historical chronicles, which seemed, generally, to be the most stable and permanent. Then there were what I called Great Dreams, the stories which were repeated on important days, like the ceremony of lights. Then there were Sabbath Dreams, which were more important than ordinary dreams but were not yet accompanied by much music or ceremony. Then there were the fairy tales, as I called them, amusing dreams or stories often told to the children, and sometimes told as allegories to teach some lesson on how to be a strong dreamer. Then there were the winter tales, those prepared conglomerates of each person's store of the year's dreams, then the weekday dreams, often made up of things from winter tales.

The daily dreams that each person told every morning never got to me unless they were repeated. Often they were not, though they were always acted upon, and I began to feel very uneasy about missing the vast category of what might be called pragmatic dreams—like where to plant the potatoes this year, or go to the hol-ka to get rid of impatience with the bleating of Sbgai's newest lamb.

The only trouble with my categories was that they kept overlapping or breaking down into new divisions. But I tried not to let that bother me. I felt I must simply get on with the work, trying to complete the Chronicles, Great Dreams and Sabbath Dreams, at least, during my lifetime. If I could do more than that, fine. If not, perhaps someone else would carry through the work I had mapped out.

Some of the children had begun to be curious. I stopped working in the fields and spent time teaching the children to read and write. I soon had quite a large team of young scribes who, however, lost interest after an hour or two each day. I tried to enlist the help of the old, who did little work in the fields and knew the stories better than anyone. But while they would help if asked, they never volunteered and showed no interest in learning to understand the writing. The young adults and middle-aged politely refused to have anything to do with the work, and I assumed that they felt someone had to do the field work. I agreed with them. After all, we could not all stop work to do this.

Augustine worked in the fields in the morning and met me for our usual noon interlude. But in the afternoon she disappeared completely. I discovered she spent most of the afternoon in a hol-ka.

"Is something troubling you?" I asked her. "Do you feel ill?"

She shook her head and smiled so that I would not be concerned. She did not speak much, but then she never had.

I went on with my work, and the seasons passed. The seasons passed and the work grew. The more I did, the more I saw to do.

After the next winter fast, Augustine moved out of our ka. At first I was upset, but she explained, with tears in her eyes, that she had dreamed many times that she must leave the ka, was stuck in that dream and could dream no further. She feared disobeying it any longer. "But our time at the river will continue," she said.

I got used to this arrangement more easily than I expected. After all, at night we slept. I missed seeing her first thing in the morning, but I looked forward to every noon. And in our grove, nothing changed. It only got better.

Augustine's move had no effect at all, that I could see, on our daughter, who behaved as if every adult were her parent and every child her brother or sister. She was extraordinarily bright. She could already read the skins and often stood watching me write.

I noticed that Augustine did not stay long in the ka she had moved to. Her dreams seemed to dictate that she stay only a few weeks and then move on. "Eventually you will work your way back to us," I said. She no longer went to the hol-kas at all, and I never saw her enter one again. In the afternoons she sat, in various places, seemingly at random, as still as if she were in her winter trance. Yet she still managed to get more work done than anyone else, and was always available if someone wanted her.

The scope of my work grew, as did the number of categories: history, customs, ceremonies, allegories, fairy tales, songs, health practices, agricultural methods, bodily disciplines, etc., etc. I could see no end to the work, and I was happy. I could hardly wait to get to Augustine at noon to tell her about a new part of it I had projected for someone, sometime in the future, to do.

In addition to directing more and more of the planting, Augustine was beginning to do healing. Instead of going to a hol-ka when feeling out of sorts, or after an accident, people went to Augustine, who touched them briefly, almost apologetically, as if she were embarrassed. I saw one child whose foot had been cut by a bone tool. A few minutes after Augustine touched her, the wound was closed and there was hardly a mark to show where it had been.

But after that time Augustine refused to do any healing. It was quite definitely donagdeo, she insisted.

"Why?"

"Each must heal himself."

"But when I came here you all healed me."

"That was different."

But she more than startled me at the next ceremony of lights. When Augustine reached the Life Tree and stood looking at the children dancing round it, the branches of the tree suddenly burst into flame. It was not my delusion; everyone saw it. The tree blazed for a moment; then the flames sputtered out. Augustine looked as surprised as the rest of us. But we all turned to look at her, all feeling that somehow she had caused it. She hung her head and looked embarrassed again, and, of course, everyone but me turned aside and pretended nothing had happened.

"Did you do that?" I asked.

"I don't know."

"How did you do it?"

"I don't know. Please let us not speak of it. It is unimportant. It is nothing."

"Nothing! I think it's pretty impressive."

"No, no. Whatever it is, it means nothing, nothing at all, like a trick. It is more fun for the children to be lifted up to light the tree anyway."

"You thought of it alight, and it lit up."

"Anyone can do that; it is nothing."

I saw my work broadening again to include feats like this one. Of course, the others had done things like this too, though not so dramatic: the taming of animals, the hypnotic disappearance of the island. I hadn't thought much about those things, but I realized now that if I were sensitive to them, I would probably notice more. I promised myself that in the spring I would set a group of children to observing and recording such phenomena.

I almost lost my helpers when I did this. They considered the work so boring that few would spend more than a few minutes on it. They were far more interested in recording dream material. So I set aside such work for a later time, when, as Chil-sing assured me, some dream would send a willing worker to me.

I had never been so happy in my life. As we were storing the seventh harvest since my arrival, I put my arms around Augustine and said, "If anyone had ever told me that happiness was monogamy, primitive living conditions, and absorption in a work too vast to be completed, I would have laughed." I did laugh, but with joy, for Augustine had come back to our ka to spend the winter. I felt sure she was back for good.

Five

My hibernation was fretful and restless. I still did not dream, but I had a sense of dreams taking place behind some kind of veil. Each time I woke, I saw Augustine in her trance. I don't think she slept at all during that whole winter. She became very thin, and I could hardly get her to take any food at all. I spent a great deal of time awake trying to feed her, and, when I slept, I tossed and strained to see things I could not quite make out.

But spring came early and gloriously, the first day with dazzling brilliance and a great burst of grass and blossoms. I wakened Augustine from her trance and helped her up, taking her hand and leading her outside.

People were coming by on their way to the la-ka. They all stopped for a smile from Augustine, and were especially happy after passing her. I don't think I had ever seen such a joyous spring on Ata. Everything glowed. Even the sun seemed new, brighter than I had ever seen it.

After the others had passed, we followed, and soon we

were all in the la-ka, sitting on the still slightly damp steps with the sun streaming over us as the mats torn from the roof blazed in the fire below.

The oldest one knelt before the fire supported by the children as we all quieted down.

"Has any kin been chosen?" Silence.

"Has any kin been chosen?" I waited for the third repetition of the phrase, eager to celebrate the beginning of what would be such an exciting year. I squeezed Augustine's hand.

"Has any kin been chosen?"

Augustine released my hand and stood up. I grabbed her hand and tried to pull her down. A great moan swept over the la-ka. Augustine said nothing. She simply stood there looking into the fire. "No," I said. "What is this?" My words were drowned out by the moaning, which broke into sobs. People began to sway uncontrollably. Augustine moved. I tried to grab her, but Salvatore stopped me. Tears ran down his face as he shook his head at me. Augustine walked down the steps to the fire and stood in front of it.

The moaning gradually died down, and the people fell into silence. All went forward onto their knees. Augustine stood very still saying nothing. The silence deepened. There was finally no sound at all, not a rustle of wind, not a crackle from the fire, not the sound of a bird, not even the buzz of a fly. No one breathed. It was so still that I swear I could hear the rays of sunlight pouring over Augustine. Then that sound stopped. For an instant all was as still as if the universe had stopped.

In that instant Augustine walked into the fire.

I screamed, leaped and fell down the steps, and would have thrown myself in after her, but Chil-sing grabbed me. He was stronger than I now and easily held me.

"Please, you will be hurt."

I went on screaming, I guess. I don't remember much except that people were holding me, people who were weeping. I cursed them, I called them savages, I screamed, and sometimes I just panted. I wanted to die. I learned later that three of the old ones died when Augustine walked into the fire.

I awoke in a hol-ka where I lay trying not to think, hoping it had all been a nightmare. I smelled herb broth, felt around, found a shell full of it. I thought of spilling it on the ground and dying there in the hol-ka. But I didn't. I grabbed it and drank it down, coughing and groaning my anger. My rage would keep me alive. I crawled out of the hol-ka and walked back to the la-ka in the dark.

Everyone was still there, of course, and Salvatore was seated on mats near the fire, talking.

"Savages!" I cried as I staggered in. "Despite everything you're still savages. Human sacrifices. Is there anything more inhuman? Your animals don't even do that. You killed her, as surely as if you'd pushed her in. The best of you, and you killed her. Under this veneer of dreams and gentleness, you're keeping cruelty and savagery, ready to leap out on your best."

No one bothered to look at me. They all sat like crumpled rag dolls, with their heads hanging, tears falling. They ignored me as one ignores the extravagant but sincere mourner. I looked all around, and I could see nothing but grief. I had never seen these people give way to such misery. It was real, as real as mine, and I could say nothing more against them. I sat down, hung my head like the rest, and cried.

Salvatore went on talking. He was speaking words of a ritual I had never heard before. It was not like the funeral rituals I had witnessed. They were brief, almost casual, and actually joyful, since to these people death meant only release into their dreams. This was more like a funeral, a funeral for a person who'd gone to hell.

" . . . guard our Augustine through her sufferings and keep her always in the dream. Let her not be overcome. If she must suffer, let her sufferings be brief. Let them be such as she can bear, yet less than that, or let us in our dreams and in our waking life and work, bear them with her. Help us in our loss. Let those who mourn be comforted. Let us not poison our dreams with grief. Let us get on with the dreaming, else this sacrifice will be in vain, and strengthen us to . . . "

This went on all night until the fire died.

In the morning, when the ashes had cooled, I went into the fire pit. I searched the ashes, sifting them through.

"You will not find anything," said Salvatore.

"The fire wasn't that hot," I said. "The skull, part of her, some part of her is here."

Salvatore shook his head. "She is not there."

"Yeah, sure, she's in dreamland."

"You do not understand, my kin. She has not died. She has gone to your world. She has been chosen. You know the story. You have written it on the skins."

"She walked into the fire. I saw her."

"No, she did not walk into the fire. The fire only helps

us to concentrate, only stands for the . . . " He shrugged as if it were hopeless to try to find words for what he meant. "Before her foot touched the fire she was gone."

"Why?"

He shrugged again. "To save us. To save all. When kin waver on the brink . . . "

"What will she do there?"

"I don't know."

"She'll never come back?"

"But of course she comes back."

"When?"

"Every day. If not every day, often. In our dreams."

"But I don't dream!" I yelled at him.

"My poor kin, perhaps you will."

"If she comes back to you, in your dreams, why do you all mourn so?"

"We mourn for her, for her sufferings, for the suffering she has been chosen to take on herself."

"What suffering?"

"The suffering of living in your world."

"Haven't you any idea what she will do there? Will she be a seer, a prophet, a . . . this is a bad time for prophets in the world . . . "

"It is always a bad time."

" . . . they lock them up in cages there. Will she be the founder of a religious cult, followed by a bunch of neurotics and laughed at by everyone else? Will she . . . " I thought of Augustine—black, female, in that world run by men like me. "Sbgai said a great philosopher of that world was one who went back."

"It is possible. But most often, those who go back live very obscurely, lest they fall into the temptation of talking too much, of fame and admiration, and of belonging to things. The suffering of living in that world is not the worst danger."

"But if she lives the life of a poor, obscure black woman, what good can she do? If what you say is true, it's a waste, a terrible waste!"

Salvatore only shrugged. He went to the fire pit and began the seven days history and rededication of Ata.

During those days and nights I wandered around the island like a lost man. I did not sleep, and I ate little. Round and round in my head whirled the question of what to do, what to do. My goat followed me, silently at my heels or jumping ahead of me when we climbed the hill.

On the last night of the spring ceremonies we climbed the hill together. We sat in the fresh new grass on top of the hill, and I put my arm around the goat's neck. "What'll I do, eh?" I said to the goat, who promptly folded her legs, nuzzled against me, and went to sleep. I curled up with her, closed my eyes and dozed off. And for the first time in years, I had a clear, vivid dream.

I was in the London Underground. It was all clear, the musty, hot-air smell, the grimy tile walls, the posters advertising women's underwear and opera. I walked from one tunnel to another, people rushing past me, hurrying somewhere. I wandered slowly, aimlessly, not knowing where I should go. Trains rushed into tunnels and stopped. I watched the people crowd on and off. I got onto a train, rode for a while, then got off and wandered through another station, and another, and another, aimlessly getting on and off trains which rushed me to places but not to a destination.

Then I was on an escalator. It was one of the oldest ones, with dirty wooden steps, a great steep escalator that went from the depths of the underground up to the street level. I seemed to ride slowly upward for hours. I could not see where I was going, and I was suddenly alone, the only person on the long escalator.

Then I reached the top, and, stepping off the escalator saw the sign WAY OUT ahead and above me. I walked toward it. Standing under the sign was a ticket-taker, a black woman in the usual dark blue uniform. She smiled and held out her hand. I looked at her face and saw that she was Augustine.

I jumped awake, shivering with cold. The dream had been so vivid and clear, more clear than what I saw in the early dawn light. I hurried down the hill and ran to my ka.

"I have dreamed," I said, and told my dream to Chilsing, who was now a robust young man with his golden hair tied back in a woven cord. He smiled happily when I mentioned Augustine and began at once to tell everyone that I had seen her already.

I thought about the dream for the rest of the day. I could hardly wait for night, and after the last "nagdeo" was said, I closed my eyes and waited. And waited.

Of course, I was too tense to sleep for a long time, and when I did fall asleep, the sleep was shallow and dreamless. I kept waking up anxiously asking myself if I were about to dream. This went on for several nights.

"Am I trying too hard?" I asked Salvatore.

"Perhaps. Under tension, even if you can dream, the dreams are of little use."

"What should I do? Tell me how to dream better, Salvatore."

He smiled broadly and stretched himself. "My kin, I have waited a long, long time to hear you ask me that question."

"Then you must be ready with the answer."

"There are many answers. Not THE answer. I can give you some answers, but not all." He settled himself, sitting cross-legged, and his speech slowed, as if he were thinking and considering very carefully everything he said. "Simply to dream is not enough. There are many, many kinds of dreams. They exist perhaps on different levels.

"There are the simple dreams that tell us of a body need. If we are thirsty, we dream of drinking or if we have eaten too much we dream of someone standing on our stomachs. (Yet to dream of thirst when your body is not thirsty is something else entirely—but I do not want to speak of that yet). These simple dreams tell us much and are very valuable. Especially if they tell us something we would not know when awake, some inner strain or beginning of dis-ease that we should correct.

"Yet, no one is content merely to have such dreams. So we try to live in such a way as not to make these warnings necessary; each person must find what is the right amount of food, drink, work, as if to keep a rhythm going, a dance, in which some imbalance causes us to miss a step in the dance. We try to live so as to get beyond these dreams, and to get beyond them we must obey them, or we must dream them until we do.

"Other dreams tell us deeper things about ourselves. These are not simple dreams any longer. Sometimes they are very direct and sometimes veiled, but they come only after the simple bodily dreams go. And it is even more necessary that we obey them. For instance, your dream of writing was such a dream that had to be obeyed, why, I do not know. But as you advance, you will find that the messages of the dreams become less direct, as though the higher messages find difficulty fitting into a language that will reach us.

"Then there are the dreams in which we open ourselves to other people, dreams in which we find that the words and gestures, the crude and indirect ways of our waking life, are not necessary. That we can be touched more directly. That we can listen and see better. Such a dream as the one you had last night."

"You believe I received a message from Augustine?"

"I do not know. We can never be sure. Do you believe it?"

"I must."

"Nagdeo!" he congratulated me. "Belief in the dream is as important as emotional discipline. Then there are dreams . . ."

But I interrupted him. "No, first I want to know how to have that kind of dream again."

"But I have told you."

"But I already had the dream. After being sleepless and hungry and all the things that should make me have trivial dreams."

"Yes, you leaped ahead. You have done this before. But you have not repeated the dream, or gone on?"

"No."

"And what does that suggest to you?"

"That it was a freak, a suggestion, just like, get a drink of water. A suggestion to turn toward dreams and learn how."

"Perhaps. A still higher kind of dream is . . . " But I

waved him away, and he fell silent. "Just as well," he said with a smile. "Too much talk . . . "

" . . . is donagdeo." I laughed and gave him a little salute as I walked away. I wanted to learn this ESP dreaming or whatever it was. I was too impatient to listen to much more theorizing about dreams.

Yet, even at that point, my whole life had made a complete shift, a greater change than had been made by my coming to Ata. For a long time my life had centered around Augustine and the writing. Now that she was gone, Augustine was even more the center, as the WAY OUT.

I had no doubt that I could learn how to get to her. After all, I had seen stranger things than that on Ata.

Salvatore had said that every man must find his own path to higher dreams. Searching for the path and trying to stay on it is absorbing and vital to the man who tries it . . . but I doubt it would be of much interest to my reader. Furthermore, if I were to set down the specific things I discovered about my own progress in dreaming, I might be guilty of making rules or laws, which, as soon as they are frozen, become violations of the spirit behind them.

Since I lived on Ata, there were no physical barriers to my progress in my surroundings. Ata provided the conditions and the freedom to choose or not to choose to live according to the universally accepted dream regulators: a simple diet, enough physical labor, few distractions, the company of people with shared values, solitude when desired.

I soon discovered that the real challenges lay beyond the acceptance of these material conditions, that no adherence to dietary or work regularity made up for the loss of rhythm resulting from an angry word or a malicious thought. But I have no time to explore such considerations here.

Let me merely summarize those next few years by saying that I learned that for me the best schedule was to get up at dawn and work in the fields until noon. Then I went to the grove where Augustine and I had spent so many hours. There I rested quietly and thought of her. After half an hour I went to the village and worked on the skins. As the sun began to lower in the sky, I went to a hol-ka where I spent the hour before sundown. Then I followed the others to the la-ka, where we fed each other and listened to the stories or watched the dance. It was now that I began to participate in some of the dances, which at first were very difficult for me, but which I found helped to create the harmonious disposition that often led to an especially vivid dream of Augustine.

I very shortly began to see her every night. She worked in the London Underground for a year. Then she worked as a servant in France. Menial work serves as a passport to anywhere. I followed her from country to country, always moving south, until she reached South Africa, where she stayed for a brief, terrible time.

Australia, New Zealand, then the orient, going north, then east across to Japan, then South America: she circled the world on her knees, scrubbing floors of the powerful, succoring the oppressed. Gradually she worked her way north to the States, where she settled for some time in the South.

I could see her, but she did not again look directly at me or show in any way that she was aware of my witnessing her. It was as if there were an invisible wall between us. I tried various ways to break through that wall by varying my routine, my work hours, my time spent in a hol-ka. But I could not get through to her. I could only watch.

She never lost the rhythm, the grace of her dance. Her most menial chore became a part of it. Every morning she rose and spoke as if she were telling a dream to someone, and when she was not working she sat in trance. I could never hear a word she said.

People gathered round her as they had on Ata. They kept getting between us. Finally at the end of every day she was alone. But then it was morning, and I woke up. My frustration became unbearable. "There's some sort of time difference; it's day where she is when it's night here," I told Salvatore. "I see her in her daily activities, but I can't dream with her at night." I tried reversing my sleeping hours, but that didn't work at all. I simply stopped dreaming.

Then one night I saw her working in a restaurant in what seemed to be a northern city. She stood behind a cafeteria counter taking orders for food. I stepped up to the counter and tried to say something to her, but she interrupted me. "You cannot order anything," she said very firmly. "You must accept what is offered here."

It was the first time she showed by any sign that she knew I was in touch with her, seeing her. The next morning I told Salvatore about the dream and asked him what it meant.

"What do you think she is telling you?" he asked.

"Patience," I said with a grimace. But I did not feel patient.

About this time Jamal and some of the other teenagers

discovered that eating the petals of a certain flower would induce the most vivid and exciting dreams. For several weeks he and a few others lay about laughing or exclaiming excitedly. The adults ignored them, but I was intrigued with their discovery and determined to try it to see if it would speed up my progress.

The effects were dramatic. When I entered Augustine's life, she was practicing songs in a small store front church. She immediately recognized me and threw her arms around me. I was ecstatic as I began to talk to her. But she did not want to talk. She began to pull off the cheap print dress she was wearing. She ripped off my tunic, and on the alter of the little church, she pulled me down upon her, to make love. But it was not making love, it was the practice of sex, such as I used to practice, a repertory of chilling incitements, mechanically performed. Her movements were precise and machine-like and they began to speed up, faster and faster. Her face gleamed in a sweat of lust, and her blue eyes turned red. I woke up screaming. Salvatore was standing over me.

"That wasn't Augustine!" I insisted. "It wasn't."

"Right, my kin," he said soothingly. "It wasn't."

"It was the flower. The flower did it. You must warn the people against it."

"No warning is necessary. It is discovered and tried by nearly every generation. And then it is not touched again."

It took me a long time to get back to the point where I could see Augustine clearly again. I was not tempted to try any more short cuts. In fact I was so chastened by this experience that I became especially careful to watch what the best dreamers of the island did, and to try to learn from them. What I learned was simple: more patience, more stillness, acceptance. They had, as they put it, nothing to teach me, and that "nothing" was everything.

At first faintly, then clearly, but still at a distance, I followed Augustine again. She remained in the United States. Now I patiently endured the people who came between us; though their appearance was hard to bear after my years on Ata, I began to look at them.

Their faces and bodies were ugly with dis-ease. They were petty and cruel and destructive. I wondered how I could ever have wanted the admiration of these people. I began to see that the Atan Chronicles were right in describing them as blind men before a banquet table who starve because they cannot see the food in front of them. The more they suffered, the more terrible things they did to escape suffering, thereby causing even more suffering.

Yet in all of this, I began to see acts of true kindness and love which shone like the jewels I had first seen in the la-ka. It was as though, from time to time, some people caught a glimpse of the life they had left. I came to understand that everything they did, however perverted, was truly, if they only knew it, a misdirected attempt to regain Ata. After watching them, following Augustine for over a year, I could feel nothing but pity for them . . . and even love.

And at that point the breakthrough came. I was resting by the river in our grove, thinking of Augustine. Suddenly she was there, just as she used to be, lying in my arms. I was afraid to move or to talk. I only hoped that she would stay. I held my breath. When I let it out, she was gone.

Again, I will not detail the daily progress I made toward keeping her with me for longer and longer periods. I do not think that I can explain the process in words that would make any sense to the reader. Let me make an analogy to the dance again: so long as I kept a certain rhythm, moved to a certain music, in everything I did, she was there throughout my waking activities, as surely and as clearly as she had been before. Anything that broke that rhythm—anger, impatience, sometimes just talking—and she began to fade away.

What began as a desertion was now a fuller closeness than we had ever had. At night when I slept, I watched her and stayed with her in all her activities, and now she saw me, acknowledged my presence, and welcomed it. During the day, she stayed by me for as long as I held the rhythm, and I bent all my efforts toward prolonging those times.

But do not think that the skill of keeping her with me was permanently gained. It too was like the discipline of the dancer. I had it only while I practiced; each day brought a new beginning of the discipline, and any period of disuse was paid for in hours of emptiness before I could regain the rhythm.

That was how seven more years passed. Life went on as usual on Ata. Kin moved in and out of our ka, keeping a more or less complete sleeping wheel. Chil-sing matured to the age I had been when I came, and showed signs of being a strong dreamer. Sbgai's great lumbering body moved more slowly, but steadily. Some babies were born. Some old people died, Aya among them. When she died, Salvatore began to age very rapidly, as though hurrying to catch up with her and join her.

My daughter seemed to spin through life, like an

amber top. She had left our ka when Augustine went back and, though she came to help me with the skins, she avoided me otherwise, as though wary that, since her mother had left, I might come to depend too much on her. She would soon reach womanhood, as a desert blossom that suddenly bursts upon the world. Soon the blossom would become fruit; she would have a child and end this spinning. Then, perhaps, she would start to glow, as her mother did.

I spent those years following Augustine and telling of her in the ka. I began a skin, telling of her activities, to add to the Chronicles of Ata.

She worked hard at menial tasks and kept little for herself. What she had, she gave where it was needed. She sang in poor store front churches and brought great comfort to miserable people, but she and her songs were also in the front of protests against injustice, and many marched to her song. I was always beside her, hoping to help with whatever strength I could give her, but feeling always that it was I who drew strength from her.

Always there were more and more people around her. Crowds began to come to hear her sing in church; political groups asked her to perform. Whenever this began to happen, she packed her few things and moved to another city, another housework job, another storefront church. This was how she kept her anonymity.

What more is there to say to describe those years? They were happy ones, but not in the mindless, childish ways of the ones before. We learned to be together in almost every instant, and we rose to love which shares pain.

At the end of the seventh year she was killed, by frightened men in a senseless riot. They had set dogs upon her, but the dogs refused to touch her. A young man raised a rock to throw it, and she stepped in front of him. She was shot.

I knelt over her as she lay on the street. "You were to show me the way out," I said, without speaking.

"That is what I have done."

"Don't leave me, Augustine."

"I will never leave you." And she was gone.

I told it in the la-ka that night, as I had, for all those years, told everything she did. We walked in procession to the high cliff where the dead are left, and we waited for the sunrise. And when the light came up from the water, I knew Augustine was in it, and I was glad that she had been freed from her ordeal and allowed to go Home.

I no longer saw Augustine, either waking or sleeping. And, remembering what she had told me when the old Frenchman died, I did not try to call her back. I kept the rhythm with as much patience as I could, desiring nothing, trying not even to desire to see Augustine. Whether or not I could see her and touch her, she must be there. She had said she would be.

At this time we ran out of skins. I had written on everything possible. Most of my helpers had lost interest, but new children took up the bone pens each year and learned to make scratches. As they matured, they left me, as my daughter had at about the time of Augustine's death.

I had run out of skins precisely at that point where I envisioned an even greater expansion of the work. For after years of collecting the dreams of Ata I had been more and more intrigued by their similarity to mythology, folklore and literature of the outside world. For every version of every Atan dream there were scores of corresponding versions in the outside world. I had an idea that if I could reconcile all versions from the outside world with the several Atan versions, I would arrive at some greater truth behind them. If, in fact, I could manage to do this with only one dream, in all its multiple expressions, that effort would be a worthwhile project to fill the remaining years of my life.

But where to write it?

Immediately I had a clear dream in which I saw the stone wall covered with carved writing. I took this to mean that, reluctant as I had been to labor so tediously, I should begin to work on the stone wall. I told this dream to Salvatore in the morning, and immediately went out to begin. He followed me and watched.

I began to wash and scrape down a portion of it. When I had it quite clean, I felt and examined it closely to see what kind of tool I would need for etching into the stone. That was when I began to see a pattern in the scratchings. For the next few days, I scrubbed and scraped sections of the wall, finding the same patterns, faint and eroded, but clearly there, and clearly like the markings I saw in my dream.

Salvatore sat silent, watching me.

"Did you ever notice these markings before?"

He nodded.

"What do you think they are?"

"What you think they are, my kin," he said gently.

"How long have you known they were there?"

"For a while. I too saw them in my dreams."

"Was your dream like mine?"

"No, there was more to it."

"Tell me."

"In my dream the people of Ata began to make markings. They were very pleased, believing that all the great dreams of Ata would be captured and preserved, and none would be lost. They wrote on skins, on clay, on mud. They even wove the stories into the mats. Finally, because all these things decayed and were gone, they carved the stories into the stones of the wall, and the stones of the hol-kas. I think that if we take a light into a hol-ka we will probably find better preserved markings in the rocks.

"But then disputes arose as to which were the best versions of the dreams, and as to whether the mark gave the correct meaning. Many more marks were invented, and many worked on carving alternate stories. Kin split over which story was correct. Which should be carved and preserved? There was no time to carve all the stories; choices would have to be made.

"But even more serious was the effect that writing had upon the words of the story. It froze them. People began to mistake the word for the unknown behind it. Instead of expressing the unknown, the carved word became a thing between the people and the unknown which it should symbolize.

"All was donagdeo. The people ceased to dream high dreams. And so, one by one they stopped the writing and the reading. They went back to the old way of telling the dreams in spoken words that rose like smoke and disappeared into the air to intermingle there, where there was room for an infinite number of dreams, which could change and grow and become closer to the reality."

"That sounds," I said, "like a part of the history of Ata."

"Yes," said Salvatore. "It was lost for a long time, up there in the air, but it has come back in our dreams when it was needed again."

"Why did you wait to tell me?"

"I spoke it in the dawn. You did not happen to hear."

"Why, didn't I listen?"

"We can only hear what we know."

"And only see what we believe is there?" I pointed to the stones of the wall. He laughed. We sat down together and laughed. I saw how futile were my attempts, my categories, my agonizing over the choice of a word, my attempts to fix permanently something that was alive and must grow. Even the children had known better than I; they put it behind as they did other childhood games when they began to grow up.

"Why do you suppose my dreams told me to write for all those years?"

"Who can know? For some reason important to you."

"I thought I was writing for the others, for all kin."

"Perhaps."

"No. I was writing for myself. Maybe to make the dreams of Ata a part of me . . . running them through myself as water rains down and filters through the earth."

"Perhaps."

We stopped talking and laughed again. Laughter was better than words; silence better than both.

I left the skins as they were. We unrolled them and used them to cover kas or to wrap babies against the winter cold.

That winter I slipped into trance and remained quite warm, needing little food.

And now I began to dream steadily and richly. I learned that there are levels of dreams far higher than I had imagined, higher than anything Salvatore had told me, higher than could be expressed, even in the language of Ata. But some I could express. I dreamed new versions of the stories I had written down. We added them to what we already had, as I told them in the la-ka, letting them rise "like smoke" into the rich atmosphere where there was room for all signs and symbols of the reality that was there though we did not see it, as Augustine was there though I did not see her.

Seasons passed, but I no longer kept track of the number of cycles through which we lived. Time was one; there was only now. I dreamed by night and sometimes by day. I kept my rhythm, thankful for each day that I was able not to fall too short of nagdeo, especially considering the kind of man I am. I felt Augustine everywhere now, yet not as I did before, but her essence, like traces of her in the air, in the people, the animals, something that was and was not Augustine, but was becoming something greater than Augustine, something purer, now that she was released.

In the afternoons, after the field work, I told the children tales, remembering the ones I had written and elaborating upon them from my dreams or from ideas that sprang into my head while awake. In the river grove I discovered a new kind of herb, one that no one on the island could remember seeing before. I had seen it in a dream, found it where Augustine and I used to lie, and knew that it should be added to our spring broth.

I was grateful that I had been able finally to do one small thing for so great a people. For now I knew them as they really were, not a happy, primitive, innocent people, free from the cares of the world, but the sustainers, the sufferers who tried to counter-balance what was done by men like me. People waiting patiently since the beginning of time, resigned to going on till the end of time, knowing that they could look for no great progress, no sign of the coming fulfillment of their dreams. People who gave all their strength to the most strict, self-imposed, unarticulated discipline, resigned to maintaining this balance, and the balance of the whole insane world, until it would, of its own choice and from its own realization of necessity, come back to Ata.

It was only after living among them for so long that I understood the greatest miracle of Ata. It was this: that the people were no different from any other people in the world, subject to the same faults, desires and temptations, but living each day in battle against them.

My summons came very quietly during a winter trance. It was not spoken in words, so it cannot be translated.

On the first bright spring day, Salvatore, fragile and hairless, looking rather like Aya, knelt in front of the fire and asked, "Has any kin been chosen?"

At the third, "Has any kin been chosen," I felt myself rising without my own will. I heard the moans of the people as I walked down the steps, fixing my eyes on the great fire. I stood before the fire until the silence deepened and deepened, until the universe stood still and I heard the unspoken, "Now!" And I stepped into the flames.

Six

"He's pretty badly burned."

"What's in the I.V.?"

"Just dextrose and water. For dehydration."

"Has he come around at all?"

"No, but then he's under heavy sedation."

"Pulse?"

"Pretty steady."

I could distinguish two men's voices and one woman's. Then everyone drifted away again.

Sometime later I surfaced through the drugs again to hear their voices.

"I think he'll make it. How's the fever?"

"Almost normal."

"Try to get some food down him."

Again I slipped away, only dimly seeing a woman from time to time putting something into my mouth, then touching me in some way. I opened my eyes. My right leg, in a cast, tilted upward in front of me.

"We're just removing some of the bandages," she said. "There, you look almost human." She smiled at me. "Do you know where you are?"

I opened my mouth, but I had forgotten the word. I stammered a couple of times, "Host . . . hos . . hosp . . ."

"That's right, you're in a hospital. I'm your nurse, Mrs. Banner."

I nodded.

"You're a very lucky man. Those burns were pretty bad."

I didn't try to answer. Speaking English was too much effort. I lay still, thinking that I must remember to tell Salvatore that he was wrong in thinking the exile was completed before the chosen kin actually touched the fire.

The nurse went on chattering. "But you're healing so well that there probably won't be any scars. You'll be just as handsome as ever," she simpered, as if I were a young man. I wondered if that were part of the therapy. I didn't know how to respond; it had been so long since I had been exposed to anything but simplicity and honesty. "Want to see?" She picked up a mirror from the table, and held it before my face.

I had not seen my reflection during all the time on Ata. Most of the skin on my face was peeling. My eyes were still almost swollen shut. I looked thinner than I ever had been, but aside from that there was no change. One side of my head was shaved and bandaged. But the other side still sprouted thick black hair. I was puzzled, for although the people on Ata were unusually healthy, they aged the same as all people.

"Bet it'll be a long time before you feel like sunbathing," the nurse rattled on. She took the mirror away, and I closed my eyes so that she wouldn't expect me to answer her. I tried to trance, but couldn't. I lay quietly with my eyes closed remembering that I would have to wait with patience to discover what it was I was to do next. Perhaps, like Augustine, I would roam anonymously where I was needed. I felt the nurse giving me another injection, and, as I went under, I felt a fleeting doubt cross my mind: after all this time, had the nurse recognized me?

I awoke from a drugged sleep, thinking that I must refuse to let them give me any more drugs—it might take days before I could dream again. My leg lay flat on the bed now. I sat up and tried to trance, but I still could not.

"Feeling better?" A nurse got up from a chair across the room. She stretched. "I'm the night nurse. You've had special nurses round the clock, but it looks as if you won't need them anymore. Before I go, could I . . . have your autograph? My boyfriend is a great fan of yours."

She was holding out a slip of paper and a pen. I took the pen in my hand and just looked at it. Then I put it to the paper, but I couldn't write. I wanted to tell her that through all my years on Ata, I had remained nameless. I held the pen, waiting, wondering if perhaps my name would be given to me now. But nothing came.

She frowned. "Sorry, of course, you're tired." She walked out stiffly, and as she opened the door I saw a flash of dark blue uniform. There was a policeman standing in the hall outside my door. I heard a rush of voices, then a firm, "No, gentlemen, nobody goes in."

I watched the dawn gray the sky and wished I had a dream to tell to myself. In a little while another nurse came in.

"Well, you look quite yourself today. Maybe you can eat something. Right after medication." She took a small paper cup off a tray and handed it to me. It contained two red pills. I shook my head. "Come now, you must take your medication. Doctor s orders."

209

I shook my head again. "No . . . more . . . drugs," I managed. "Please," I remembered.

She went on urging and insisting but I paid no attention to her. When she finally flounced out of the room, I was relieved; although even the quiet of this place was noisy, it was good to be alone. But she was back again almost immediately with a doctor.

"Well, glad to see you up and alive," he said, uneasily. "Got some pills here'll make you well faster."

"No drugs, please," I repeated.

He gave me a kind of sneer. "I can appreciate your feelings, but these aren't drugs in that sense. They're to help you get well. You're very subject to infection right now. These pills are just anti-biotics."

There was no use arguing, no use trying to tell him that I could cure myself faster without them. The arguing would simply make things worse. I took the pills.

As soon as I swallowed them, he looked triumphant and relaxed as if he'd been worried about what he'd do if I continued to refuse. He became even friendly. "You realize what happened?"

I started to nod my head; then I knew that I should not explain how I got here. I thought it best to hear the story as he saw it. I shook my head.

"You had an accident. On Bear Mountain Road. Your car went off. Must have gone 300, 400 yards, straight down. It's a miracle you survived at all. Do you remember anything? No, I see from the look on your face . . . you were thrown clear, but injured pretty badly, bump on the head, broken leg, lacerations and bruises.

"That valley's pretty hot and dry this time of year, 120 degrees at noon. No one goes down there. It was just a lucky accident some kids found you. Otherwise you couldn't have lasted another day. As it was you were practically naked, burned to a crisp, delerious. You'd wandered several miles from the car, dragging yourself around and around in circles. They found traces. You ended up back at the car again. When they brought you in, we didn't think much of your chances; after three weeks of that, we were surprised to find you breathing. Amazing, the recuperative powers of a young body. Remember anything?"

The door opened. "Don't say anything!" A man rushed over to the bed. It took me a few minutes to get him straight.

"Spanger," I said, my lawyer, H.P. Spanger.

"He doesn't remember anything," said Spanger to the doctor.

"Apparently not," said the doctor, with a sneer that turned into a shrug of indifference. "He's still not allowed visitors."

"I won't stay long," said Spanger.

"Five minutes," said the nurse.

Spanger watched them go, then turned to me. "What do you remember?"

I couldn't answer. I couldn't think at all.

"Listen, I've gotten you out of plenty of messes, but it'll be a miracle if I can get you out of this one. Try to pull yourself together, and, remember, don't talk to anyone. Don't say anything to anyone. This place is crawling with reporters and every nurse gets two cash offers an hour for any quotation.

"You know a girl was found dead at your place?" He looked at me as if holding his breath. "That's right, just keep that blank look. You don't remember anything. You don't even know who the girl could be.

"The girl is named Connie Catlin; that's her stage name, real name Janet Complenz. She was found dead, strangled, in your bedroom. No one could find you. Neighbors said they heard a quarrel. Signs that you took off in a hurry. The search was all over the newspapers. Here." He pointed to a stack of papers he'd put on the table. "The longer you were missing, the worse it looked. You were convicted in those papers. Then they found you, almost dead. For the first time there was some doubt in their minds. You could have gone away on a trip and let the girl use your place. Or you could have quarrelled then left. An intruder, caught robbing, could have killed her."

"Time's up." The nurse held the door open determinedly. The cop behind her sneaked a look in at me.

"Okay. I'll be back to talk to you again when you feel strong enough. Until then I advise you not to talk to anyone."

It wasn't real. Nothing was real. I can't describe the shock that hit me. For about three days the doctors felt I would die after all. You know the story of Rip Van Winkle. This was worse. My loss was infinitely more than the few years lost by the old man in the story. He had slept, while I had awakened. And was I now to find that my awakening was only a dream?

I lay without speaking for two weeks. I tried to sleep to let dreams through. I saw only shadows, like the old shadows of long ago. They did not frighten me any more, but when I tried to face them, to make them visible, they only shrank into nothing. I could not trance. I had lost the rhythm; there was no unheard music to move to. There was nothing.

"You're not trying," the nurse began to say, and the doctor signed a release for me to leave the hospital. I refused to go. My lawyer came every day, thrusting the newspapers under my nose. "Listen, right now, temporarily, you've got a bit of sympathy on your side because of the accident, but it won't last. We've got to get a hearing on this thing right away, while you're still in a cast. Pull yourself together, man, your life may depend on it."

I finally read the papers. I will not repeat their contents, as probably you are familiar with the case. I would only say that the newspapers, in vilifying me, in giving long accounts of my squalid relationships, my excesses, my other violent episodes, culminating (as they correctly guessed) in my killing of Connie, did not exaggerate. The only thing that bothered me about the accounts was their underlying flavor of envy and admiration.

"They're really out to get you," said Spanger. "They can't forgive you for doing all the things they wish they had the guts to do. Now, listen, if you're not going to end up dead or in a cell for the rest of your life, we have to move fast, now!"

I felt dead already, or too heavy to move. I could not imagine that I had been sent back to be caged or killed as a murderer and forgotten. What good could that do?

Once I had asked that question, all certainty fell away from me. I lost everything.

A good look in the mirror showed that I was thirty years old, no older. The dates on the papers, the statements of my lawyer, showed that no more than a few weeks had passed. I wished with all my soul that this were a dream, and I waited and waited to wake up. But I did not. Had all the events of the past time happened? Did Ata exist? The answer was obvious: Ata existed, but only in the drug-laden and injured brain of an admittedly imaginative and desperate man.

Once out of the hospital, it was impossible for me to cling any longer to the hope that anything had changed. I had undergone some profound experience. Perhaps it had changed me. Perhaps some day I would understand it. But in the meantime, Spanger convinced me, I had to survive.

"Your leg, and the trouble you have speaking because of the head injury, that's all right, that's good. I think it'll gain some sympathy at the hearing; there'll be a grand jury hearing first. It's just possible we can convince them that you left and someone else came in and killed her. That's what happened, isn't it?"

He showed me more newspapers. Their tone had changed slightly. There was a possibility that I was innocent, a possible mystery murderer, and my miraculous survival. To sell newspapers, it was expedient to be somewhat more sympathetic to me now. My lawyer hoped to take advantage of this. "After all, you're a pretty famous man, not a common criminal. Sale of your books has tripled. If you come through this, if a lot of people begin to see how much money can be made off you alive and writing again . . ." He crossed his fingers and grinned.

I stayed at home and waited for the day of the hearing. I sent the servants away, and hobbled around, eating whatever I found—there was an incredible amount of food and liquor in the house, more than I could consume in a year. I lived with the lights out and the drapes drawn to keep out the people who crept about the place, trying to get a look at me.

Spanger advised me not to answer the phone, saying that if any friend wanted to see me, he would contact Spanger. No one did. But I knew that after I got through the hearing, if there were not enough evidence to try me, there would be dozens of "friends" and scores of women, just as there had been before . . . only a few weeks before.

And I would be more famous than ever. And there would be more money. And any trash I wrote would sell, for at least the next three years, until a new sensation was found. By that time I would have enough money to live in ease for the rest of my life.

I signed the statements Spanger brought to me.

I sat in front of the unlit fireplace. I tried to drink. But the wine soured in my stomach. So I just sat until the day of the hearing.

"They will already have read a lot of documents, evidence presented by the district attorney and so forth. You probably won't have to say much. Just being there willing to talk, looks good. You've a good presence, and you look a bit strung out yet, and the crutches help. Direct your words at the women, you know what I mean. Our strongest argument will be that a man of your intelligence could not have been running away from a killing. Simply by reading your books, people know you've got too sharp a mind to do anything like that."

I looked around the large round table at which these people sat informally, almost apologetically, sneaking looks at me, as they would at any celebrity. They were leading citizens of the city, respectable and respected. And ugly with pain. How I longed for the beauty of the faces of Ata.

As I watched them shuffle papers and glance at me, that ache grew into intolerable tension. I felt as if I might snap or explode. I felt faced with something so momentous that the whole universe was at stake.

The hearing would probably decide my survival. But, of course, survival meant a return to my old life. Since I now cared little for that life, I could not imagine why I felt full of this intolerable suspense.

I tried to analyze my situation calmly. Rationally, I had two choices.

I could, if lucky, carry through this lie about Connie's death, and return to my old life . . . perhaps with resolution not to live it quite the same way, though it might be hard to keep a resolution which started with a lie.

Or I could tell the truth, be sent to my death, or to jail, still living out my life, but in considerably less comfort—in fact, subject to cruelties which might make me more vicious than I had ever been.

Those were the two alternatives, and between them the first seemed the only intelligent, rational choice.

But what if there were a third choice? What if, against all reason and evidence, against all common sense, against all rationality of the most intelligent or practical mind . . . what if Ata, the dream, was real?

What if, for some very good reason as yet unknown to me, I had been sent back not only in space, but in time. If I were willing to believe I could be sent through space, why did I balk at the possibility of being sent through time? Was one more difficult to believe than the other?

If I had truly been sent back, if there were the slightest chance that it could be true, I would have to discipline myself to find the rhythm again, just as I had done when I was trying to contact Augustine. No matter what happened to me, no matter how hard the material events that came upon me, they were not real, if Ata was real. And, conversely, if I could not begin with belief in Ata, how could I ever find it again?

There was only one way to find out if Ata was real; that was to believe, to do only what was nagdeo, even if it meant throwing away my life. It was a gamble with all the odds against me. If I lost, I would die or spend the rest of my life in a cage.

Suddenly I laughed; would that life be any less vicious a prison, any less a death, now that I knew what it meant to be an Atan? With that laugh, the tension loosed its hold on me. Or, rather, I let go, like the last letting go in a long series of surrenders.

My laughter attracted their attention. Everyone looked at me questioningly. A couple frowned disapproval of my laughing at such a time.

"The statements. The statements I signed," I said haltingly, "are lies. I killed the girl."

To describe what happened next is, I am beginning to believe, impossible. I have written it over and over again, but it is still not right. If I had a whole lifetime to rewrite and rewrite, I still could not get it right within the limitations of words. And time is running out, so I must ask my reader please to accept the following as a suggestion of what actually happned, and to believe it.

There was an instant of silence, a silence more profound than that of the dumbfounded people around the table, more profound than the dark silence of the hol-ka, more profound even than the silence in the instant before I stepped into the fire.

And then there was light. Indescribably warm, glowing light. Light was everywhere. It shone on everything, through and into everything; it came out of everything, out of everyone. It was like a fire that does not consume, but not like a fire, like . . . like nothing else, nothing else was like it. But all things were full of it. The faces around the table, the table itself, the walls, the windows, everything was alive, everything lived in and through the light.

And I too. I too. From the center of my being the light broke in waves, in orgasmic waves, outward to the extremities of my body, every cell of my body melting together in the waves of light that flowed outward from my center, and over me from the very air around me, from everything. I breathed it into me and it poured out of me, sweeping through me like a million orgasms. I was full and whole. I was part of the light and of all the other things that shone in and with the light. All were one. And whole.

In that instant I understood all the stories and dreams and songs and dances of Ata, stories of jewels and of sun, of fire and of ocean. I understood the many versions of each story and the contradictions and paradoxes, and I knew that they were all, in their own way, true. For I had glimpsed the reality behind them.

Tears blinded my eyes for a moment but did not fall. Blinking through the blur, I saw something fluttering down from the chandelier above us. It circled my head once, then lit on my shoulder, a small black moth.

I have not spoken since then. There is no time. I know

now why I was taken to Ata and why kept there and why chosen to come back. It was to fulfill Augustine's dream by shining this feeble light on the people of Ata. What I don't understand is why it should have been me. Perhaps I was chosen because my career, my life, my trial and my execution will attract a larger audience than might come to read the book of a better man or woman.

The guilty verdict and the death sentence came quickly. Spanger, confused and disgusted, went through the motions of pleading me insane. But an ambitious young assistant district attorney introduced a dramatic surprise: evidence for premeditation, in a letter Connie had written to a friend. In it she said she might be pregnant and planned, not an abortion, but a paternity suit demanding a huge and continuing share of my income. Then he read from one of my books, which details how a clever murderer feigned catatonic insanity and escaped prison. As he read to the court, he pointed to me, where I sat in trance most of the time to save energy so that I could write all night. He said I had been observed writing at night and insisted, quite rightly, that I could hardly be catatonic, yet able to write when I thought I was not being watched. He convinced the jury that I hoped to cheat the law and then publish a book which would capitalize on the trial publicity. And many people came forth to testify to my dishonesty, violence and opportunism. I bear resentment toward none of them. They merely told the truth.

While in trance I was attended by my daughter, who witnessed my trial, telling its events at dawn in our ka, to which she has returned. From her I learned that Salvatore died in the effort to send me back, and that his place and mine in our sleeping wheel will be taken by her and by the baby she carries in her body.

I would prefer to spend my remaining time with the people of Ata, but I have had to work night and day to finish the book in the time left to me. I have had to leave out many things, and even those that I have told may be misunderstood, told, as they are, in the faulty medium of words, and frozen on paper.

It is finished and tomorrow I go Home.

Perhaps you picked up this book because of the sensation surrounding my trial. Yet, you must have wanted more than sensation or you would have thrown it aside before now. If you continued to read, it was because in this hasty and incomplete account, I told you something that at some level of your being, you already know. Something you know as an echo, as a glimpse in a dream or as a fragile hope you are ashamed to voice.

Do not judge these words by the man who writes them. Listen, not to my words, but to the echo they evoke in you, and obey that echo. And think that if I, a murderer whose murders were the least of his crimes, if a man like me could find himself in Ata and could re-learn the dream, and further, could glimpse for a moment the reality behind the dream . . . then how much easier it might be for you.

You have only to want It, to believe in It, and tonight, when you close your eyes, you can begin your journey.

The kin of Ata are waiting for you.

Nagdeo.